The Current That Carries

The Current

FLANNERY
O'CONNOR
AWARD
FOR
SHORT
FICTION

Nancy Zafris,
Series Editor

That Carries

STORIES BY **LISA GRALEY**

THE UNIVERSITY OF GEORGIA PRESS ATHENS

Paperback edition, 2018

© 2016 by the University of Georgia Press

Athens, Georgia 30602

www.ugapress.org

All rights reserved

Designed by Kaelin Chappell Broaddus

Set in 10.5/13 Arno Pro Regular by Kaelin Chappell Broaddus

Most University of Georgia Press titles are
available from popular e-book vendors.

Printed digitally

The Library of Congress has cataloged the
hardcover edition of this book as follows:

Names: Graley, Lisa, author.

Title: The current that carries : stories / by Lisa Graley.

Description: First edition. | Athens : The University of Georgia Press, 2016.

Identifiers: LCCN 2015047529| ISBN 9780820349879 (hardcover : acid-free paper) |
    ISBN 9780820349886 (ebook)

Classification: LCC PS3607. R3495 A6 2016 | DDC 813/.6—dc23

LC record available at http://lccn.loc.gov/2015047529

Paperback ISBN 978-0-8203-5472-9

For my mother and father and brother

and in memory of

Esther Eleanor Lovejoy

(1924–2010)

as form in sculpture is the prisoner
of the hard rock, so in everyday life
it is the plain facts and natural happenings
that conceal God and reveal him to us
little by little under the mind's tooling.

—R. S. THOMAS, "Emerging"

CONTENTS

ACKNOWLEDGMENTS

From my earliest years, I have loved stories. I'm grateful to my mother, Joyce, for wonder-filled library books in the summers of my youth and to my father, Paul; my cousin, Elaine; and a host of other relatives who have always been in the habit of telling and listening to stories on front porches. I recognize with love, as well, my brother, Michael, whose constant camaraderie lent itself to our rich, imaginative childhood together. I appreciate the love still kindled on the home place.

A special thanks goes to Harold Edwards from McCorkle Elementary, and Pauline Rymer (now deceased), Betty Prunty, and Julian Martin, from Duval High School, teachers who introduced me to literature and whose nonjudgmental acceptance of marginalized people still matters to me.

Additionally, I'd like to thank Marshall University professors Rainey and David Duke, who acquainted me with the likes of Ivan Ilych, Gregor Samsa, Anne Moody, and Julius and Ethel Rosenberg, characters and people to whom I still give considerable thought.

Beyond this, I'm indebted to graduate mentors Robert Olen Butler, John and Carol Wood, Darrell Bourque, Marcia Gaudet, and especially Mary Ann Wilson for their instruction and continuing guidance and friendship. As well, I cherish the friends who have been readers of my stories and tellers of stories themselves, among them Maryclaire, Joe, and Jeff from newspapering days; fellow writers from McNeese State University: Pam, Neil, Amy, Tacey, Ron, Kay, Dave, Nadine, Adam, Mike, Steve, and Celeste; and colleagues from the University of Louisiana at Lafayette: Christine, Elizabeth, Jennifer, Lydia, Monica, Randy, Yung-Hsing, Susan, Jenny, Kathy, Felicia, Ian, as well as other colorful souls in Griffin Hall and on the UL–Lafayette campus. For the fellowship of all these people, I am heartily grateful.

To my entire Lafayette family, Lisa and Mark, and most of all Taylor —whose big-sky love and big-sky faith hourly light my vision—I express my thanks for refuge, sustenance, and companionship, as well as my love for their *being*.

For giving me the time to write and shore up stories in this collection, I extend my gratitude to the Louisiana Board of Regents for an ATLAS (Awards to Louisiana Artists and Scholars) sabbatical. It made an inestimable difference. Here I make mention, too, of my abiding esteem for the Friends of the Humanities in Lafayette for their enthusiastic support of literature and the other arts.

Finally, I give a heartfelt nod of thanks to Nancy Zafris, series editor of the Flannery O'Connor Award; the folks at the University of Georgia Press for their professionalism and kindness; and Barbara Wojhoski for her meticulous copyediting.

Several stories here have appeared in literary journals including "Crossing with Sassafras" and "Vandalism" in *Glimmer Train Stories*, "Feeding Instructions" in the *McNeese Review*, and "The Sorrows You Can't Enter" in the *Georgia Review*. To the editors of these journals, I am certainly appreciative.

The Current That Carries

VANDALISM

They were at it again. You could hear them way up at Ray Marker's. First there was a loud, ear-splitting crack—sharp lightning to a tree—then the reverberation of aluminum, like someone slamming the lid of a washing machine. You could almost feel the bat vibrating in your hands.

Denzil sat in his underwear on the edge of the bed with his shotgun. He hadn't held it in years, and it was heavier than he remembered. Olive would not have approved—no matter how many mailboxes he'd had to replace. Up the road, he could hear the engine goosed, then slowed, then goosed again. He stepped to the window and parted the curtain. Through the brush and trees, he could see the headlights as the car picked its way from one house to the next.

From his bedroom he tiptoed to the front door. There was no reason to be quiet, but Denzil was quiet out of habit. He turned the deadbolt gently, opened the door, and slipped out onto the porch. Tiger Boots squeezed out behind him. There was a chill in the air he hadn't expected, and a large harvest moon waxed in the southwest sky. He kept forgetting it was October, past time to gather firewood for the porch. Lately, his impulse to stock up and maintain had lost its urgency. There comes a time when you want only to sit on your porch, he told Glenn Turley. You want to think over the things you've done or haven't done—not the things you're planning to do. The car sped closer and closer, and as it rounded the curve, it swerved toward Glenn's driveway.

Denzil was late with his shot—it was drowned out by the solid whack of the bat and Glenn's mailbox scuttling on the road—like someone dragging a muffler. Denzil aimed again, for the passenger window, and stayed the course as the driver gassed the car and lurched toward his own mailbox. If they could feel the spray, Glenn had said, maybe they would stop. Denzil let out his breath, eased the trigger, held the gun steady, and braced for the kick. He felt the cat going around his legs.

Luck was with him, and he heard the scattering of rice on the windshield and the side of the car, then a screech of locked rubber on the pavement. The car skidded into the post of his mailbox—he heard the splintering of wood and winced. Last time he'd just had to replace the box. Don't let them, don't let them—he was thinking—slide on over into the creek. But even as he wished against it, he watched it happen, the rear end of the car sliding around first, then going down, so that the front end, when it was over, pointed straight up the bank toward the sky.

"Daggone it," he said under his breath. "Daggone teenage drivers." It didn't take much to put them in a tailspin. He imagined three or four sweaty seventeen-year-olds on his couch later, wringing their hands, while he called their fathers—if there were fathers. The kids would make the kinds of vows you always make under pressure, the kind he himself had made in their shoes back when tipping outhouses was the mischief your father sat you down for.

Suddenly, the dome light came on in the vehicle, and Denzil heard the radio, something with a bass line that jarred the porch floor under his sock-footed feet.

He took his gun and went inside, Tiger following. He dialed Glenn's number.

"You all asleep?" Denzil asked.

"How do you sleep through that?" Glenn asked.

"They're down in my creek."

"Oh, brother," Glenn said. "Turned over?"

"No. Right side up. Probably busted something underneath though."

"I'd like to bust something," Glenn said.

Denzil heard Dorothy's voice in the background. "What's she saying?" he asked.

"She says I'm liable to bust something I don't want, if I'm not careful."

Denzil laughed. "She may be right."

"What we need?"

"Winch, I guess."

"I'll bring my jeep," Glenn said. "Hey?"

"What?"

"Try and scare them till I get there."

"I'll try." Denzil could hear Dorothy's voice in the background, and he put down the receiver gently. Tiger was on the couch now. She had worked her head under his hand, while he peeked out the window. No one had gotten out yet. He hoped the wreck had done the job of scaring them—and that he would be left only with the task of consoling.

He turned on a lamp in the living room to let them know someone was awake and then went back to the bedroom for his pants and boots. Tiger followed him room to room.

"It's not morning yet, kitty," he said. "I'm not feeding you." In the kitchen he turned on the light. His cereal bowl from the evening was still on the table. It wasn't that he couldn't cook, he'd told his daughter Missy, just that he didn't want to. Why make extra work?

From the cabinet over the refrigerator, he pulled out a couple of six-volt lanterns, nearly tripping over the cat. "You been up on the table?" he asked, but the cat went around his legs, avoiding the question. "I said I'm not feeding you."

When he stepped back onto the dark porch, the cat followed. "Stay and guard the place," he whispered, scratching once under her chin. He heard them down in the creek trying the engine. It sounded like the intermittent coughing of a sick goat, something wedged in its throat. Maybe the engine was flooded.

On the top step, Denzil paused, wondering if he should take his shotgun, but an empty gun, he knew, was worse than no gun. Climbing down the steps, he felt autumn in his knees and ankles. Out from under the roof, the air was crisp—crinkly. He filled his lungs and smelled the leaves on the lawn and then wood smoke, too, someone burning the first fire of the season. It was the first year he didn't have anyone to burn for.

Down through the yard, he let the moon guide him. It was bright enough to cast his shadow. They were just boys looking for fun, he knew. On Fridays, the week loosened, it unwound itself. That was just the way of it. He remembered how it felt. You had an energy, looked around for a place to put it after bottled-up days of school or even work. It was why his father always started planting or plowing up potatoes on Friday evenings. House painting. Bridge building. Bringing in the hay. Ditch digging. Anything to keep him home.

Down on the road, Denzil felt more strongly the vibration of the car's radio. The bass got mixed in crazy with his heartbeat, made a kind of pulse in his head. With his thumb, he clicked on a flashlight mid-swing, shone it toward the car. It was a ninety-one or ninety-two Camaro. Would be hard to pull out without tearing something more, the way these cars hugged so close to the ground. Already, he was sure, Mr. Louisville Slugger was bobbing his way down the creek. And probably a case or two of beer had been thrown over, too.

The voices in the car were arguing. "Shut up and get out."

"I ain't getting wet," someone said. "It's your friggin' car."

The car was at a steep angle. Denzil shone the light in the driver's eyes. "You boys okay?" he asked. The driver's pupils were large—as he had known they would be—even with the light. But he was young, younger than Denzil expected. Denzil smelled beer, maybe something else in the air, he wasn't sure what. It was strong, though, and his mind flashed to the craft room at vacation Bible school. Maybe he'd helped some of these boys when they were little. Denzil saw there were four of them. Lying back in their seats, facing the sky, they looked like astronauts in the cockpit ready for blast-off.

"We're okay," the driver said. He was normal-looking enough. Clean-cut hair—kind of wet-glistening, light-colored, sticking straight up like new grass sprouts. Just one earring, a tiny one. The boy on the passenger side leaned over and turned off the radio. Denzil shone the light to all their faces. One boy in the back had blood on his face, probably from getting thrown against the seat when they crashed.

"You all right?" Denzil asked, holding the flashlight on him.

"I don't know. I think my nose is broken."

Denzil recognized his grandson's voice—even nasally—before Elliot's face registered through the blood. A zigzag tremor ran from Denzil's head to his heart, triggering a string of questions whose ends were cut off by the beginnings of other questions. He felt the kind of disorientation you feel when a dish from the kitchen winds up in the toolshed. He clenched the flashlight tighter, wondered what he ought to say. But Elliot covered his face with his hands and turned his eyes away.

"He's all right," the boy at the passenger door said. Denzil shone the light back to that boy. He was probably the bat boy but wasn't as big as Denzil had imagined. Maybe that was the cause of it all, that he was a squirt and needed to prove something. His hair was short except in the front where his long bangs came down and curled away from his eyes like a ski jump you'd see in the Olympics. He had the beginnings of a mustache and a little patch of felt under his bottom lip.

Denzil saw how it was. Elliot had been given the least desirable seat, back of the bat boy where he was most likely to get clobbered by the ricocheting bat. Maybe that was how he got his nose busted.

"Your parents know where you are?" Denzil asked again, directing the light back to Elliot, whose face was still in his hands. Missy had said there was some kind of trouble with Elliot. His grades had dropped. He was staying late at school for a lot of art projects.

"I got projects," Denzil told her. "Send him over."

"You come and get him," she said. "I can't twist his arm."

Denzil hadn't known what to say to that. No time before had anyone had to twist the arms of his grandsons for them to visit.

"He's tired of being in his brother's shadow," Missy continued. "He quit the football team."

"He's not one to push—not like Danny," Denzil remembered saying. "He's tenderhearted. Like his grandmother."

"Not just his grandmother," Missy had said.

For a moment, no one spoke. Then the driver said, "Maybe you can help us get out of the creek?"

"What? Now you go'll make an old man push?" the one in back with Elliot asked. His head was shaved bald.

Denzil stepped back from the car. He shone the flashlight all along the bottom of the car. "I dunno. Looks pretty bad. I guess you better go sit on my porch. Let me call a wrecker."

"No, man. No wrecker. Are you out of your mind?" The driver opened his door. He had to push hard against gravity and the weight of it. "We can get it out ourselves."

"You can try," Denzil said. He watched the driver squeeze out like he was releasing himself from a spring-lock trap. The driver looked back inside. "Get out, you bunch of morons," he said.

"I told you my door's jammed," the bat boy said.

"Get out on my side," the driver said. He strained to hold the door open for them. There was a rocking of the car, and one by one, the boys climbed out and made their way up the bank onto the pavement. They had on baggy jeans. The boy in back with Elliot had green tattoos on his arms—snakes or something with long tails. All the boys were scrawny. Not the bruisers Denzil had imagined. In their too-big pants, they reminded him of cornstalk scarecrows, the kind Olive made for the porch at Halloween when the boys were little. Elliot, with his promising big feet, was the runt of them all. That was what happened when you took kids away from farming. No wrestling with heavy bales of hay, no buttermilk, no biscuits.

"Oh, wow," the bald one said. "That was some ride. Some ride. I mean friggin' Camden Park. My heart feels like it's going to come out of my chest."

"I think I'm going to be sick," Elliot said. He bent over and vomited on the pavement. Denzil felt sick, too, a heartburn that radiated out to his fingertips.

Elliot wiped his face on the sleeve of his T-shirt.

"Maybe you better come inside, let me see about your nose in good light," Denzil offered. "I used to drive for the VFD."

"I'm all right," Elliot said.

"I think you're supposed to put your head back to make the bleeding stop," Denzil said.

"What do you know about it?" Elliot asked.

And then Denzil saw how he was supposed to play it.

"Come on," the driver said. He led the boys down over the bank toward the rear of the car. Elliot went with them. Denzil heard a splash. "Shit," one of them said.

"Quit crying, candy-ass," someone else said.

When Denzil was their age, not many boys talked like that. You weren't raised that way. He guessed they did it to impress each other. It was hard to get used to, but maybe TV made it easier. He moved down the bank sideways, getting his footing carefully, and held the flashlight for them. He had heard of people, in wrecks, having superhuman strength. He watched now to see if it would be true of these skinny boys. The bank was steep. The car was nearly straight up and down.

"Don't let it tip back over on you," he yelled down. He listened to their straining and groaning. Good for them to work out some adrenalin. He hadn't planned on them being so quarrelsome. He looked up into the woods for Glenn's headlights but saw no sign of him. It was too late for anyone else to be out.

Denzil held the lantern, flicking it occasionally from one boy to the next. Without better light, he couldn't tell if any of them, besides Elliot, was worth saving. It was hard to tell a boy gone bad from one who was just learning his way. If he could detect a preference for any one of them on Elliot's part, he decided in the darkness, he'd do his best to help them both.

"Don't you have a tractor or something?" the driver yelled up at him. "You could pull us out."

"Well, I dunno," Denzil said. "Looks like you're wedged in pretty tight."

The driver stepped out of the water and climbed part way up the bank. He opened the car door, squeezed himself in, fumbled around, then brought out a lit cigarette. "Let's take a break," he yelled to the others. He came up the bank to where Denzil was standing.

"Look here," Denzil said, leading him to the front of the car. "Looks like you're hooked on my mailbox post for one thing."

"Like a friggin' fish," the driver said. He sucked deep on his cigarette, held the smoke. Denzil shone the lantern for the boys climbing up the bank. Their wet shoes squished on the pavement. Elliot was not with them. Denzil heard him vomiting again, down in the creek. He wondered if he would remember catching minnows there with Daniel. Or floating wooden boats Denzil had helped them build when the water was high. The boys would chase them with sticks from one end of the creek to the other, freeing them whenever they snagged. Running with sticks made Denzil nervous. Be careful you don't put an eye out, he'd told them. One summer Denzil brought home a tractor inner tube, taller than himself, and blew it up with his air compressor for Daniel and Elliot to float on. It looked like a giant black donut. There was nowhere to float to—since the inner tube took up all of the largest fishing hole. But Elliot would lie back for hours and let you spin him around and around, sometimes with his eyes closed and sometimes with them open to the swirling trees and clouds above him.

"Your friend down there may need a trip to the emergency room," Denzil said to the driver. "I wouldn't mind to take him."

"You were shooting at us," the driver said, taking another deep drag. "Why was that?"

Denzil had been working out an answer to this in the minutes while he held the light, in the minutes while he was remembering Lonzo Loftis and the spontaneous combustion of his outhouse just as he and Glenn and Romie Moore had crept up to it. Only time he ever saw Glenn Turley running scared, but later Glenn claimed he was just pretending.

"I was aiming to use dynamite," Denzil said. "I could string a fuse up to the porch, wait for you to get close enough, then blow the mailbox sky-high to heaven." The other boys stood listening. "And you all with it," he added, just for bragging points with Glenn.

Denzil felt their collective attention.

"I still might light a match, throw it back there at your gas tank," Denzil said. "I brought some just in case." He reached in his pocket, took out the little box of matches, shook it. "See?"

Denzil felt the driver's hand come around his wrist. The suddenness of it scared him. With the other hand, the driver snatched the matchbox. "Are you crazy?" he asked. "Ellie's still down there."

"I'm up," Elliot said, mounting the top. "What was he doing? Trying to kill us? Over a little old mailbox?"

"It's true it don't bring much these days," Denzil said. "Just duns."

"Just what?" the bald, tattooed one asked.

"Duns," Elliot said. "What old people call bills." Denzil felt the sting of the words and a second sting, knowing they'd been aimed to hurt him.

"He's just bluffing," the driver said, blowing out, long and slow, the way of characters in crime movies.

"Be one way of getting your car out," Denzil said. The cigarette smoke, what he had given up years ago for the sake of Olive and the children, was pleasing to him. He was taking chances he wouldn't have taken with Olive alive. But he didn't know how far he could go. Maybe the trick would lie in dividing them, separating the fearful from the brave.

"You say your parents are expecting you?" Denzil asked again.

"Listen, you fat bastard," the driver said, whipping down his cigarette to the pavement. "You're going to go get your tractor, and a chain, and pull us out." Denzil felt the cold, hard end of something—he guessed handgun—against his temple.

He swallowed. "It was just rice," he said. "I was just shooting rice."

"Well, I ain't just shooting rice," the driver said. "So you'd better do what I say."

What Denzil thought—*you think I'm afraid of some Mickey Mouse pistol, you'd better think again*—he didn't say. He pulled his lips together, concentrated on the half-smoked cigarette burning on the pavement at his feet. He would curb the tide of courage he'd been riding. He felt in the boys now what he had been hoping for—reverence and awe for the situation at hand. But he hadn't expected it to take so much. The shotgun would have raised the stakes considerably, and he was glad he hadn't brought it.

"I know a guy with a winch," Denzil said. "Lives right up there." He nodded his head the direction of the woods.

"Let's just get your tractor," the driver said, pushing on Denzil's head with the gun, "and not bring anyone else into it."

"I'll go get the key," Denzil said, but he didn't move, waiting for permission.

Elliot groaned. "I gotta lay down." He sat on the edge of the pavement, then leaned back.

"We better get him to the doctor," Denzil said.

"What do you care?" the driver asked.

"I care," Denzil said. He wanted Elliot to hear.

"The tractor," the driver said. "We're gonna go get your tractor."

Denzil didn't want to take the boys to the garage. He didn't want them to see what tools there were to steal. "Better just let me go alone," he said. "Don't want to wake up everybody."

"Who's in there?" the bat boy asked, stepping closer.

"Well, my wife, for one," Denzil said, trying to think of who else he might name.

"Is that right?" the driver asked. "Maybe she'd like to make our acquaintance."

"Bet we can give her some things you can't," the bat boy said.

"No, man," the bald one said under his breath.

"She's dead," Denzil said. "My wife's dead." He didn't like saying it, but he didn't like the direction things were going either. He didn't like Elliot hearing this talk. Elliot had stayed away when Olive was sick, even during the bouts of remission when the prognosis looked good. "He's just being a boy," Denzil had said to comfort her, but it was Elliot's absence that told them how hard he was taking it.

"You probably killed her," the bat boy said, "crazy old loon."

Denzil heard the crunching of gravel and saw Glenn's headlights high in the trees. He needed to get some kind of control back before Glenn showed up. But it was hard with the gun pointed at him.

"You don't need the gun," Denzil said. "I'll help whatever way I can."

"Maybe I like having the gun," the driver said. "It's like a security blanket." He took the gun from Denzil's head, pointed it at his own face, put the muzzle to his mouth, and kissed it. Denzil grimaced. He wondered what they were high on. He wondered how deep in Elliot was.

The gravel crunched louder up on Glenn's driveway, and Denzil felt the boys hearing it.

"Who's that?" the bat boy asked.

"That's Glenn," Denzil said. "The guy with the winch."

"Now we're talking," the driver said. "You mind you don't try anything funny."

At the bottom of his driveway, Glenn stopped, then got out of his truck. He walked into the headlights, kicked something, picked it up. Then he got back in, eased on down the road, and slowed at Denzil's bridge. When he pulled off the road, he caught them in his headlights. Then he switched on the rack of fog lights on top of the jeep. The whole creek lit up.

"Jeez," the driver said. "It's like Jeminy Christmas?" He put his gun in the back of his pants.

The jeep door swung open. Denzil held his breath. He saw Glenn carrying a rifle and something else. Always one to lead with a strong hand.

"What's going on here?" Glenn asked.

Denzil waited to see if the driver would reach back for his gun. But he didn't.

"They had an accident," Denzil said. "Need to borrow your winch."

"That right?" Glenn asked. "These wouldn't be the same ones clipped off my mailbox, would they?" Denzil saw the motion of Glenn's arm, hurling something toward the creek, saw the silver flash of mailbox in moonlight, saw Glenn, silhouetted in the headlights of his jeep, raise his rifle, heard the shot, saw the fire from the muzzle, heard the solidity of hit on the tin of the mailbox. He had to admit it was impressive.

There was an echo, then two or three more on the hills around them, as if Glenn had split the night itself and driven it, momentarily, into separate corners.

"Good grief," Elliot said from the pavement. "They're just friggin' mailboxes. Twenty bucks tops at Walmart."

Denzil swallowed. He felt sweat trickle down under his arms. Elliot didn't grasp the evident gravity of their situation. "I don't think it was them," Denzil yelled to Glenn. "Matter of fact, I know it wasn't. I hit your mailbox on my way home. Had a little too much to drink. I'll buy you a new one." Denzil didn't like the sound of his voice, but he knew the high-pitched tremble conveyed to Glenn what he needed to know.

Already he'd told more lies in front of Elliot than he'd told in his lifetime. He wondered now, what would have happened if, when seeing Elliot's face in the car, he had just said, "Hey. Don't I know you?" Now that it came to him, what he could have said, he marveled that he hadn't.

Glenn stood still. He was deciphering and making adjustments.

"Look, mister," the driver said. "I want to use your friggin' winch. I want my friggin' car out of this friggin' creek. I want my boys and me on the friggin' road in fifteen friggin' minutes."

Denzil felt the driver's arm against his own as the driver moved his hand behind his back. Denzil held no illusions about grappling with him. He was too old to fight—and had never been much of a scrapper. He didn't want the gun to go off. He didn't want it to hit anyone. And he didn't want Elliot back in the car where the gun and the gun-holder would be.

"You won't need that," Denzil said low. "He'll do what you say."

"Tell him to put his gun down," the driver said.

"Glenn, go put your gun away and come help these boys get back on the road."

Glenn began walking backwards, toward his jeep. Denzil saw him put the rifle inside. Then he got in, took his time shutting the door, then started the engine. Finally, he inched it toward them.

The driver stepped away from Denzil and went to stand over El-liot. Denzil swallowed, his pulse pounding in his ears. By the light from Glenn's jeep, he saw the driver bending over Elliot. Denzil was afraid of any funny business with the gun. He stepped closer.

"Get up so you don't get run over," the driver said. "Come on." He reached down for Elliot's hand.

"I just wanna lay here."

"No. Get up, man. I don't wantcha to get run over." The driver bent further, extending his reach, and Elliot held up his hand, allowed himself to be lifted.

The driver ducked under Elliot's arm and helped him stand.

"I got a porch swing he can lay on," Denzil said. "Be outta the way."

"You wanna lay on this fella's porch swing?" the driver asked.

"No," Elliot said.

"Just for now," the driver said. "Till we get the car out."

"I wanna help push," Elliot said.

From somewhere, the driver pulled out a white handkerchief and started wiping blood off Elliot's face. He spat on it to rub off the dried blood, and when that didn't work, went to the car and brought back some kind of water bottle that he squirted on the handkerchief. Denzil didn't know why care was so long in coming, but he hadn't expected it at all. Amazing, too, that any boy these days carried a handkerchief. His grand-sons didn't. But then their father had failed them in every way.

Glenn positioned his jeep so the lights shone on the Camaro and got out. Denzil wondered if Glenn was wearing his flak jacket under his heavy coat. When their eyes met, Denzil looked away. He didn't know what kind of signal to give and didn't want to give the wrong one or one that might be misinterpreted. A lot rested in the balance.

"First thing is we need to chop down the rest of the mailbox post," Glenn said. "I got an ax in my jeep."

"Don't you think we can jack up the front, shove the car off?" Denzil asked. The boys stood listening.

"The car's already high on the post," Glenn said. "I don't think the jack will go that high. We could try."

"No, you're right," Denzil said. "Go ahead and start chopping."

"What about a chainsaw?" the bald, tattooed one said.

"That's good," Glenn said. "I got one of those, too."

"He's like friggin' Rambo," the bat boy said. "Prepared for everything."

"Not everything," Glenn said, pleased.

He jerked the starter a few times, revved up. Then stopped it. "You boys will have to hold up the front of the car, keep the weight off the post so it doesn't kick back on me."

Without questioning, the boys gathered round, got their hands under the front of the car. "Don't get in a strain," Glenn said. "It'll take some time."

Denzil looked for Elliot and saw him lying on the pavement again. He wanted to go to him but needed to hold the lantern while Glenn sawed. The chainsaw whined in the night, and Denzil inspected the scrawny boys, doing their best to keep the car from weighing down on the post. In the sagging waistband of the driver's pants, he saw the gun, a wonder it didn't just slide on down. Denzil considered going after it but didn't know if the other boys had guns. He didn't want them to feel threatened. Every now and then Glenn gassed the chainsaw hard. The heady scent of oil and gasoline rose. The chainsaw spat out streams of confetti. Finally, Denzil saw the post wobble. He knew Glenn was through, but the post didn't fall. Glenn shut off the chainsaw, grasped the post with both hands, worked it loose, and pulled it free. He handed the post to Denzil. "There's your first piece of firewood," he said.

"Thanks, buddy," Denzil said. "Always looking out for me."

The driver reached down to pick up Glenn's chainsaw. He had to take an extra step forward to help with the weight of it. "Could do some real damage with this," he said.

Denzil saw Glenn cinch his mouth into a quick smile. "Hand me one of those lanterns," Glenn said, avoiding Denzil's eyes.

He took the flashlight down over the bank, shining it along the car's edges. He got down in the weeds, looked under it. Every now and then he flicked the light in the windows.

"What's he doing?" the driver asked.

"Deciding which direction to pull," Denzil said.

"I don't like him snooping around."

"What you got in there you're so worried about?" Denzil asked.

"None of your business."

"Don't worry," Denzil said. "He's not the cops."

"I never been in a wreck before," the bald, tattooed one said. "It's some kind of rush."

The bat boy spat. "That's nothing," he said. "One time I flipped three times. Was like being in a rock tumbler."

By their slurred words, Denzil could tell the boys were wearing down. But the long night would go on. He didn't know which ones of them would last. He didn't know if he would. He hadn't been sleeping well. The bed was colder than he was used to, and in the late hours, he fretted about vandals on the loose.

"You need to keep your friend awake," Denzil said to the driver. "In case he's got a concussion. You don't want him slipping into a coma."

"He ain't got a friggin' concussion," the driver said. "Trust me."

"What's he got then?" Denzil asked.

"Too much of a good thing."

"What good thing?" Denzil asked.

"None of your damn business."

Denzil felt the meter running. He reached in deep, tried to find another coin. It had to be sound. Finally, he said, "He seems to trust you."

"Why shouldn't he?"

"No reason not to, as far as I can see," Denzil said.

"Would you trust me?"

Denzil took a deep breath. *'Bout as far as I could throw you,* he was thinking. "Sure. Why wouldn't I trust you?"

"Because I pulled a gun on you," the driver said. "You shouldn't trust somebody who pulls a gun on you. Because," the driver drew his words out with seeming pleasure, "you never know when he'll do it again." He turned from Denzil and walked back over to Elliot, knelt down beside him. Denzil watched, heard their voices, but did not press closer.

"You all right?" Glenn asked, beside him now. Glenn trained his lantern on the back of the driver. Denzil thought he probably caught a glimpse of the gun.

"We just need to finish this," Denzil said. "Get them back on the road." He didn't mention Elliot, how he needed to keep one of them with him.

He would say that later. He hoped Glenn wouldn't get close enough to recognize Elliot till they had a plan under way.

"You think this'll run when we get it up?" Glenn asked. "Smells like it might go at any moment. What's that smell? Mineral spirits or something?"

"I don't know," Denzil said. "But it's strong."

"We can blow it up if you want," Glenn said quietly. "It wouldn't be hard. It's leaking gas."

Denzil looked in Glenn's eyes. He was serious.

"Think about it," Glenn said. "You give the signal, and we'll torch her. Be one way of putting a stop to it."

After all his years knowing Glenn, Glenn still surprised him. He'd never lost his edge, the thing about him that made him take action—instinctively—and seemingly without thought.

The driver came back. "Okay, Cinderella, what's the plan?" He looked at Denzil.

"Glenn's gonna give it some preliminary turns, see what's going to happen," Denzil said. "We don't want to tear anything up, right, Glenn?"

"The whole bottom's probably busted out," the driver said, his voice rising.

"They make things a lot tougher than you think," Denzil said. "Let's just wait and see."

Glenn backed up his jeep and chained it to a large poplar on the other side of the road. The plan was to pull the car diagonally—so they wouldn't scrape so much of the belly on the pavement at the top of the bank. Denzil knew that Glenn would be looking for a sign, for the okay to detonate it.

"Everybody ready?" Glenn stood at the winch, looked from one face to the next. He flipped the switch, and the winch began its slow whine, taking up slack. Then Denzil heard metal scraping against rock. The winch's whine pitched higher as it began the real work. More scraping. Sure to be sparks, Denzil knew. And with the grass so dry, it wouldn't take much to get it going. He thought of what the bat boy had said about Olive. He thought of the matches the driver had taken from him, like he was a child. If he had them now, he wondered would he light one and throw it over the bank.

The car rose up, scraped more. On the passenger side, leafless willows that had been lain over sprang back up. The farther up the car moved, the more hope Denzil felt in the boys. They were entranced by the slow progress of the winch and the apparent strength of the poplar that anchored the whole enterprise. *That's why we build houses out of two-by-fours,* he wanted to tell them, but he didn't think they'd hear him over the noise Glenn was making.

With the Camaro's front wheels in view, Denzil saw the chance he'd been looking for with Elliot. To the driver, he said, "Watch that it don't start to roll when he gets it to the top. Yell loud at Glenn. Make sure he hears you if it starts to roll. Don't let anyone get close."

Denzil went over to Elliot on the pavement. "You okay?" he asked, kneeling down. Even this far from the car, there was the faint scent of gasoline.

"Just looking at the stars," Elliot said. "They're spinning. The whole world is."

Denzil sat on the pavement beside him, glanced up at the sky. The light from the moon drowned out most of the stars.

"You think your nose is really broke?"

"Might be. You never can tell."

"You let me feel it?"

"No."

"You wanna sleep here tonight?"

"No."

"I want you to."

"No."

"Think about it."

"No."

Denzil didn't know when he had run out of credit. If someone had warned him, he would have been saving up. Elliot hadn't spent the night since Olive's death. Daniel hadn't either, but Daniel was away at college. He worried there was a bad seed. Their father had gone bad. Had left them and gone to another state, wouldn't even pay for school clothes.

In the darkness across the gritty asphalt, Denzil reached for Elliot's hand. It was warm but not clammy. Soft and uncalloused. Denzil lifted it—it was limp—and Elliot didn't resist. Denzil held his hand, and with his other fingers, found Elliot's pulse. Systolic, diastolic, systolic, diastolic.

How often, absentmindedly, he had found Olive's pulse, her hand in his. Or better, heard at his ear the drumming of her heart with his cheek resting on the round of her breast. No other place like that on Friday evenings. Or Saturday mornings. Eventually, most boys learned that.

Silently, he counted off seconds, and his fingers gauged the pulse against his counting. Elliot's ran in the eighties or nineties, about a beat and a half per second, high for resting but not dangerously alarming. Even after calculating, Denzil held on like he was still measuring.

By Glenn's fog lights, he saw the Camaro perched at the top of the creek bank, in the position he had hoped they could avoid, the car near horizontal, its front end on the pavement but its rear end flying out high over the creek. They had done what they could to prevent it, and Denzil didn't understand how they had failed. The car teetered on the edge. Three choices, Denzil knew. Drag it on up, scraping its underside more. Let it down to try another angle. Or Glenn's way. Denzil imagined the fireball that would light the night, the explosion sure to rock the hollow, the impression it'd make on the boys, and the pervasive heat that would blister all their faces. No way Elliot could go with them after that. It would cause quite a stir. The boys would all remember it the rest of their lives. It might even be the thing they'd tell their grandsons. But it'd scare them tonight, maybe make them think twice before going out to tear up jack. It would harden some of them, soften others. Denzil thought of Tiger Boots and the numbing fear she'd feel with the creek afire—even as far away as the porch where she waited. He thought of her, hunkered stiff in her tracks, eyes bright with blaze, not knowing which way to run. The driver, the bat boy, they would harden. Maybe enough to retaliate. What Glenn had wanted all those years ago, Denzil remembered, was to get even with Lonzo Loftis by burning his barn down.

"Listen," Denzil said softly. "This old man won't ever shoot at you again. Not for a friggin' mailbox. Not for a friggin' anything." Elliot didn't respond. "You hear me? Just squeeze my hand if you hear me." Elliot sighed, then Denzil felt his grip tighten.

He was about to go, but Elliot still held his hand. "You could have put an eye out," Elliot said.

"You're right," Denzil agreed, relieved. "It's true. Don't tell your mother."

When he got back to the group, Glenn was explaining why they didn't want to keep dragging and scraping, dragging and scraping, why they needed to start over.

"I want my car now," the driver said.

"Let's get out of here," the bat boy said. "Let's just take his jeep."

Glenn looked at Denzil. Denzil looked at the car. It made his belly hurt. He knew the longer they went at it, the more tempted Glenn would be to end it once and for all.

"One of the boys injured?" Glenn asked. "I got a first-aid kit in my jeep."

"He's sleepy," Denzil said, glancing at the driver. He felt he was in on a secret with the driver but didn't know what the secret was.

"Why don't we try one more time at a different angle?" Denzil suggested, "and if it doesn't work, we can drag it on up, scraping as little as we can."

"This is your fault," the driver said. "You shouldn't have been shooting at us."

Glenn raised his eyebrows.

Denzil swallowed, looked away. "I know," he said. "I don't know what got into me. I'll help you fix it."

"If it *can* be fixed," the driver said. Bravado had faded to pouting, but Denzil figured him still a wild card. Though he had just met him, he felt he'd been knowing him a long time.

"I'm gonna let it down slow," Glenn said. "Then I'm gonna pull it from the other direction."

By the time they got the car up and towed into Denzil's driveway, the sky along the east ridge had lightened. A few cars passed, the ones on early weekend shift. They slowed to see what morning activity another Friday night had brought. Elliot was asleep on Denzil's porch swing, and the other backseat boy was curled up on a rug. He had rolled the edge of the rug over the top of his bald head. Denzil and the driver took turns going to Elliot, making sure he was okay. Elliot grumbled each time Denzil woke him.

With the gray light, a tranquility set in—the way it will do when you are sick through the night, or sitting with someone who is sick. Denzil and Glenn and the driver and the bat boy were all moving around the car, taking turns dipping under the hood like minnows around a slice of bacon. The car, as in the night, wouldn't start. It was clear early on the boys didn't know anything. Finally, Denzil stationed the driver at the wheel and the bat boy at the driver's window so he could signal when it was time to turn over the engine. He and Glenn had their heads under the hood.

"You going to let them just walk away from this?" Glenn asked. "This might be your last chance."

"One of them is Elliot," Denzil said. "The one on the swing."

"Our Elliot?"

"Mm-hmm."

"Oh," Glenn said, readjusting a battery cable. "Tell them to try it."

Denzil raised his head up. "Try it now."

The engine clicked and wound and wound but wouldn't take. Denzil's back ached. He wanted to sit on the porch. He was tired of being under the hood.

"There's some kind of switch," Glenn said. "Some kind of impact switch. Shuts off the fuel pump."

"The inertia switch," Denzil said. He had read about it in *Popular Mechanics.*

"Yeah. That's it. You have to reset it. Where you think it is?"

Denzil shrugged, shook his head. Late-model cars were mostly a mystery to him.

"How're we going to get him away from them?" Glenn asked.

"I don't know," Denzil said. "And then, where would he go?"

"Any place be better than this."

Denzil looked sideways at Glenn. Saw the night's gray and black stubble on his chin. Saw narrow, penetrating—but tired—eyes and the face most familiar to him at the end of long, tunneled nights. He could not count the nights. More recently than even long ago. "I don't know," Denzil mused. "Would it?"

In the gap under the bottom of the hood, Denzil could see the driver through the windshield, his forehead resting on the top of the steering wheel, his eyes closed, a half-smoked cigarette hanging from his lips. The bat boy had abandoned his post and sat on the porch steps, head against the railing.

"Look here," Glenn said, quietly, nudging Denzil. "You think that's it?"

Denzil grabbed Glenn's hand before he touched the toggle switch, pulled it back. Then he reached in himself and jerked loose both ends of the coil wire—as a backup plan. He handed the wire to Glenn. "Slip it in your pocket," he said. It was the simplest thing for now. Later, when they were gone, he would unhook the wire to the fuel pump.

"You sure?" Glenn asked. "You know what you're doing?" Denzil felt Glenn studying him, the way he had the night when the doctor asked if Olive should be put on a ventilator. That was the hardest. He remembered stepping back from it, feeling amazement that hard moments came so late when all you wanted was ease for the rest of your days. He didn't talk about it with Glenn. Glenn was just there.

Denzil nodded his head. "I know," he said.

Glenn considered. "Mr. Watts," he said, lifting the corners of his mouth in appreciation. "You're full of surprises."

The fumes were strong under the hood and around the car. Denzil stepped back to get his breath, then walked to the driver's side. He felt the kind of fatigue that sticks and hangs off you like cobwebs in the fall when spiders make their last-stitch effort for winter provisions.

"Get out," Denzil said. The driver looked up at him. "Go sit on the porch. You're gonna blow your car up."

"And all of us with it," the driver said, flicking the long ash off his cigarette.

"Go smoke on the porch," Denzil said. "Check on your friend while you're there."

The driver reached in the back of his pants and pulled out the gun, held it, inhaled his cigarette. It was a revolver, seemed real enough. Looked heavy. Denzil was tired. Nights always took him through things. The driver, too, maybe.

"Put it in the glove compartment," Denzil said.

The driver ran his finger along the smooth barrel. "My father's going to kill me."

Denzil felt relief that there was a father somewhere—and that the father inspired fear. But what kind of father let his son have a fast car—and then didn't tell him how to repair and maintain it?

"No," Denzil said. "No, he won't."

In the floor of the cockpit Denzil saw the cans of spray paint and bottles of glue. He thought of the art projects. Weapons for some other kind of vandalism is what Glenn had said. Denzil said there was an awful lot of it. It was what they'd been smelling all night.

Finally, Glenn threw up his hands and slammed the hood. "I give up," he said. "I need a few hours to sleep on it."

The driver sighed and looked at Denzil. "My dad's going to sue your ass." He pulled his bloodstained handkerchief out of his pocket, began wrapping the revolver.

"I said I'd help you fix it," Denzil said. "No need to threaten me."

"You'll pay ever last dime," the driver said, relaxing as he exhaled. "I'll bleed you dry." He clicked open the glove compartment, slid the gun in, then snapped it shut.

"I won't pay a cent," Denzil said.

"You said you would." The driver opened the door, put his feet on the ground. "You're a liar," he said through the window. He looked like he might cry.

"I said I'd help fix it," Denzil said, opening the door more so the driver could stand. "Not pay to have some monkey wrench put his greasy hands all over it."

"You're not keeping my car," the driver said.

He was bound to be suspicious, Denzil knew, but he felt, too, some slack in him. "Think about it," he said. "I can fix it, maybe even throw in some extras. There's some body work needs done."

The driver shook his head, sucked on his cigarette, tossed it down.

Denzil stepped on the butt quickly, mashed it out. He turned toward the porch, left the driver beside his car. He squeezed past the bat boy and climbed the steps. Elliot and the bald, tattooed boy were sleeping sound. The bald one was rolled up completely in the rug now. Elliot lay on his side deep in the cushions of the swing. Recognizing him, Tiger Boots had curled against his belly to warm herself. The ball of the sun had just slipped full now over the east ridge, placing everything in high definition. Denzil could see dark rings of blood caked around Elliot's nostrils, but his eyes weren't bruised, his nose wasn't swollen. Denzil sat down on the edge of the swing at Elliot's head, put his hand across Elliot's brow. No temperature. With the back of his hand, he stroked the side of Elliot's face. There were hints of down, just hints still. Elliot's lips were dry and chapped. He smelled like vomit and gasoline. One of Olive's little men, as she always called them. One of their own little darlings.

Denzil felt the driver's eyes on him and looked to the driveway where he stood beside Glenn, watching. The driver knew. At some point between the swatches of light and dark and light, sometime between the winch's steady winding and the relaxing of the night, Elliot must have told him. Now he stood reading and making adjustments. Denzil waited. He would ask them all to stay. Olive had written out for him her recipe for biscuits. He leaned back in the porch swing to rest a minute and thought ahead to the breakfast he would fix them.

THE CURRENT THAT CARRIES

Dear Ron Howard, Director:

I have thought how you ought to begin with Caleb, his face the face we
see onscreen, his voice the one we hear going in—if he is willing. You
can judge for yourself after you watch him on *The Today Show*, what I've
enclosed here, already forwarded to the first mention of the story—what
Vera Lee says they call a teaser in Hollywood:

> And later on in the program, we have a story guaranteed to move your
> heart. Hear how one man's courage and sacrifice gave life to a young
> boy drowning in a river. We'll talk to the boy and his grandmother as
> well as the parents of the man who drowned while saving him. But
> before that, we have Dean Smith with the weather, and a few tips on
> summer barbecues.

Wade on through the weather and barbecuing tips—just old-fashion
common sense, not to cook too fast or too hot—and finally, you'll see a
close-up of Matt Lauer, then some footage of the shoals on Coal River,
and wa-la, you are there. First, is the interview with me—nothing flashy
in that—then the family of Guy Shamblin. We are, all of us, squenched
into new clothes, with lots of makeup and polish, so much so that Vera
Lee—that's my sister—said that I, at least, was beyond recognition. The
Shamblins, for their part, look more like themselves. Picture, if you will,

a spruced-up Clint Eastwood alongside Meryl Streep—the one angular and chiseled, the other with skin smooth as porcelain. On TV, they both look as healthy and glamorous as when they drop by for their inspections, or visits, as they say. But that is another story.

On the program, Matt Lauer is especially good with Caleb, though Caleb, on his side, weighs every word coming and going like he's in a game of egg toss. He avoids meeting the eyes of Matt Lauer—though Matt is nothing but gentle in his line of questioning.

> MATT: Can you tell us what you and your little brother and sister were doing the weekend of July Fourth?
>
> CALEB: We were all playing in the river. I was riding the shoals.
>
> MATT: Now when you say "riding the shoals," what do you mean by that? Did you have a raft?
>
> CALEB: No sir, I just rode with my body.
>
> MATT: Sort of like body-surfing on the river. Were you wearing a life jacket?
>
> CALEB: Otcher and Misty were, but I wasn't.
>
> MATT: Can you tell us what happened? When you first felt you were in trouble?
>
> MATT: I was in the long shoals, riding through. I was holding my breath, waiting to come up downstream.
>
> MATT: When did you know you were in trouble?
>
> CALEB: When I felt Mr. Shamblin pulling on my arm.
>
> MATT: Now, he was able to deliver you safely to the bank. But then what happened?
>
> CALEB: (pause, hesitation) He just washed on by.

You'll never see a more perplexed look from Caleb. He opens his hands, palms up, as if to illustrate the way Guy Shamblin disappeared. Which I guess, from his perspective, might be how it happened. But his shrug, the way he finally looks at Matt, eyes wide and eyebrows raised, turning his hands up—like *that's all I know*, or *it beats me how it happened*, or *I wish I could tell you more*—is something I've watched a hundred times without knowing what interpretation to pin to it.

Ron, when you see Caleb there, don't be surprised if you see yourself—for at that age, he reminds me ounce for ounce of little Opie Taylor—the reason I'm sending you the story. I know you'll identify with a country boy who loves fishing and swinging on old tires and who can't wait for summers so he can go barefoot. Like you, Caleb was smart for his age, a regular King Solomon, Vera Lee always said. He started memorizing the Golden Texts in Sunday school when he was just four. Seemed like he could reel in words and ideas, make them his own, then turn around, hand them right back to you. I can just picture him in front of the church commencing in on the Beatitudes, unfolding them one by one on his fingers: "Blessed are the poor in spirit, blessed are them that mourn, blessed are the meek." Some in the church thought maybe he'd go on to be a preacher as was his granddaddy—my husband, Harmon, who's gone on now. And maybe he will yet. I guess that's for Caleb and the Good Lord to decide.

He never did have the wide-eyed innocence of Opie. I tell you this from the start. I'm not trying to whitewash his life. His daddy, Layne—our son—was never associated with the sheriff, except to be running from him. And no parent, no matter how often it happens, ever gets used to a deputy's car in the driveway. This is not to say Layne was a rabble-rouser in the truest sense. But like Ritchie or Potsy or Ralph, he sometimes fell in with the wrong crowd. The difference was he didn't have a Fonzie to turn him back to the right path. Harmon and me, we done our best keeping him in the fold, but anymore it don't seem parents have the influence they once did.

There were three mouths to feed when his wife, Cindy, left, sent Layne to drinking and carrying on, then gardening things he oughtn't, and from there, it was just one thing, then another, him never in his right mind when it came to important decisions—so he made bad ones. I write this here and suppose, you being so smart, will understand what I mean. But this story—the one I'm giving you—is not so much about Layne as it is Caleb.

Caleb's been able to absorb more than his share of tribulation without visible damage. For sure, he's seen things no child ought. The worst, till the drowning, was coming across his mother with another man. Now tell me that wouldn't be enough to mark any child. It happened one Saturday when Layne had taken Caleb down to the river to fish. Cindy and this fellow climbed the ladder to Caleb's tree house and let theirselves in. When

Layne sent Caleb back to fetch a life jacket, Caleb caught them there. He was just a little bitty thing, six or seven, and of course couldn't, at that age, tell sex from violence. He thought it was a burglar had wrestled his mama to the tree-house floor. He made the awfullest racket ever was, yelling like he'd got into a yellow jackets' nest, just crying, "Help, Daddy. Help, Daddy, help," over and over like that.

When I got there—for their trailer was right next door—Cindy was on the ground trying to shush him, and Caleb stood, trembling, his hands crossed over the front of his pants where he'd peed himself. Layne come along then and was nothing for him to do but go on up and throw the fellow out of the tree house, which broke the man's leg and a couple of ribs—and a good thing not his neck.

I don't mention this as something ought to be included in the movie version, but going in, you should know the obstacles Caleb faced. He himself has not been prone to trouble—leastways not yet—though one time he stole a roll of Lifesavers from the B-Mart at Alum Creek. Just wormed them into his pocket, what the cashier said. I made him put them back, then give him the money to buy them. I've done the best I could to raise him—all three of them—and though there's always room for improvement, I don't think I was doing such a bad job before the Shamblins come along. But as I say, that is another story all together.

Ron, maybe you ought to begin with a scene or two *before* the accident—back when things were more or less as they should be. Open with a sunny day on the river. Use a blurring effect going in, so we will know it is memory, background, the foundation that the rest is built upon. You'll want to get to the point, I know—with something dramatic—but please be patient. The point will be missed if the past is ignored. Say, it's a sunny Fourth of July, back when Caleb and Misty are younger, and Layne isn't in jail. He and Cindy are making a go—she's pregnant with Otcher. They are happy, carefree. A young American family. They bring me along to fish and grill on the sandbar. At the water's edge, I help keep Misty corralled while she builds castles with her red bucket.

Meanwhile, Layne leads Caleb out to the shoals. Already, Caleb can swim, but Layne ties a life jacket around him anyway. Train the camera in close, and you'll see the kind of swimmer he is. Like an eel, Vera Lee said one time. He has a gliding ease and fearlessness. He's a natural—not because of any strength but because he can read the current and move with it.

Riding the shoals is much the same as going down a slide at one of these newfangled water parks. You shoot down, rippling where the current takes you. It's just that in the river, there's a longer stretch—in deeper water. If you go under, you wait to pop back up. That's how Layne explained it. Let me be clear, Ron. It's not the white water you see on the New River where people ride rafts. It's not nearly so fast, nor so pounding, nor so swift to change. That's not to say bad things can't and won't happen, and sometimes they do.

Here, I make reference to a letter Layne sent from jail, not long after the newspaper article:

> I believe Caleb would have got out of the current himself. He was always a good swimmer. Of course, I wasn't there. But the last time I seen him swim, we was riding the shoals like that. What it means is giving yourself up, just seeing where the current carries you. Well, we know the river can haul you a pretty long ways. But Caleb could hold his breath a long time, too. Even if he'd gone further than he wanted, he would have washed down about Web Pauley's—what we had practiced—where Web had strung his trotline, and he would have caught himself and pulled up there.
>
> Whatever else is said or done, please don't let Caleb think he's to blame for this man's death. He don't need that on his shoulders on top of everything else. Just tell him it was this man's time to go.

It's only natural Layne would think Caleb an apt swimmer since he's the one taught him. You never like to think it's your own is deficient, but everybody else. As to Caleb's not feeling guilt over Guy Shamblin's death, it would be best to let Caleb answer for it. Which, I confess, Ron, has been part of the trouble. He won't answer. We get so far along in the conversation, then he corks up. I keep hoping you will arrange an interview, just a short one even, to see if you can break through to him.

Perhaps the beginning of the movie ought to be bigger than a scene from the recent past. Men on rafts used to move timber up and down the water—before people started tossing in their washing machines and old tires. You could show how it was the river what took you one place to another. How it was the principal means of trade. Or go on further back. How it was the water what carved out the mountains and made paths, whittling away the soft layers and getting itself hemmed in by what was hard and impenetrable.

All I'm saying is I've had occasion to think about the water and its role, whether it shares in the guilt. And it's hard to blame the river, Ron, just flowing along as it's always done. You could open with the cosmic picture, the big scheme. Imagine rushing, roaring water, fast-moving streams—quick cuts, from one shot to another. Then here, slowly, is the bed the water makes, gradually meandering to the present, the Coal River, a narrow ribbon, easy-going for the most part, with shoals—like spangles—every couple of miles, and a few new waterfalls developing, signs the coal companies have been spooning in under the bed though it's illegal, and they claim never to do it.

At any rate, as you lead up to the accident, you could give a glancing shot to the day Caleb was baptized, the water hole, him wading out in his navy pants, his white shirt and a tie. Show how Harmon dunked him under, his arm around the small of Caleb's back. How Caleb bent his knees, was plunged in the watery grave, trusting he would be lifted again. No one I know of ever drowned during a baptism, and it's the same river. You'll show that the water, though menacing at times, can be life changing and purifying, too, and maybe Caleb will take it to heart when he sees the way it unfolds on the big screen.

But it's true, that on this day we speak of, the day Guy Shamblin drowned, the river was up. We'd had rain for three straight weeks—till every feature and creature that had breath was waterlogged. Everyone's seeds had rotted in the ground or washed away, that is, if you'd been able to get out and do any planting. Once the sun ventured back, we gave the river about a week, time for the mud to settle, before we set out on our picnic. Layne was in jail. Cindy was off somewhere—who knows where? A grandmother, you know, isn't the same as a parent. I knew I'd have to tighten the reins in the days to come. But on this day, I wanted them to know what fun we could have.

Guy Shamblin and his girlfriend had our sandbar. From the beginning this felt like a trespass. Every summer, we'd walked down there to picnic—just a couple stone throws from our place, see? No one else seemed to know about it. But on this day, when we got there, Misty carrying the picnic basket, Caleb carrying the watermelon, and Otcher crying because there was nothing *big* left for him to carry, they was already on the sandbar with a tent and two fold-up canvas chairs—the kind you all use on your movie sets.

Seeing them, I hesitated. For one thing, I didn't want to expose the children to any R-rated behavior. Sometimes now I think about how different our lives would've been if I had turned back. I guess it would've been different for the Shamblins, too, though who's to say now. But at the time, the children were big-eyed and expectant, longing for the first dip of summer.

"Get in and wade up the river a ways," I said. "We'll find another place."

Caleb turned to look at me, as if to say, *But here's where the best shoals are, here's where we always swim.*

"Go on," I said, gesturing with my head. All along the banks, you could see a thick web of sticks and leaves, diapers and jugs, marking the high-water line.

The children went in first, anxious to get their shoes wet. Then I climbed down with the cooler. As we passed, I said hello to Guy Shamblin, though I didn't know his name at the time.

"Hello," he said, nodding. His girlfriend sat all bunched up in one of the director's chairs. I took this to mean the water was cold. Imagine my happy surprise when I stepped in and found it warm. I stood a moment and let the water seep through my shoes—you can't go barefoot in the river like you used to, Ron, not with so much broken glass. Anyway, it struck me—and perhaps this is hindsight talking—that there was strung between the young man and the young woman a kind of stretched silence. But maybe it was entirely that they were waiting for us to move. It's one of the mysteries of the day, something to consider when you commence filming.

I guess if it was left for me to choose an actor for Guy Shamblin, I'd draw a blank. He remains a blur—though he's the one actually spoke. Time and again, I've tried to conjure him in my mind. He was not so polished as his parents—or so it seemed—standing naked but for his blue bathing trunks and river shoes. He had a lean, taut body, a boyish face, and brown curly hair. There was about him a ruggedness, but he was good-looking, too. He was young. I have marveled often just how young a life it was that was taken. He was in college, what I've learned since, studying to be a biologist. He'd had a short stint in the military. The girl would have been along the lines of Meg Ryan. She had a softness in her face like Meg that made you believe there was in her an essence of sweetness—even as she sat huddled and sullen in the chair.

When you choose actors for our parts, Ron, just show us as regular people, respectable people—though I'm inclined to think Caleb might could play himself. We don't have the shine of the Shamblin set. But we're not toothless and scraggly and lopsided neither. We have a little less, a little more, than folks around. Preachers don't have pensions—not on earth, leastways—but once I got custody of the children, the government started sending checks. Like our neighbors, we stretch every dollar till it's thin enough to see through. But we've got shelter and good heat. We grow a garden, do some canning, stock up when we can. We are never what you would call hungry.

Which is why the Shamblins' first appearance in our driveway was so startling. The four of us were sitting on the front porch, Caleb and Misty playing checkers, maybe two weeks after Guy Shamblin drowned. His father and mother pulled up in their white car—I knew it a Cadillac from the flag emblem on front. Recognizing them from the funeral, I have to admit, my first worry was they had come to collect from us—since their boy had died trying to save our Caleb.

"Good morning, Mrs. Kelly. Good morning, Caleb," Mr. Shamblin said, cresting the top of the porch steps. "Checkers, is it?"

"Yes, sir," Caleb said, not moving his eyes from the board. "I reckon it is."

"Won't you all take a seat?" I got up from the swing and shooed the cats off.

"Don't get up," Mr. Shamblin said. "We were just in the neighborhood."

"Taking a drive," Mrs. Shamblin said.

"This is the road that goes straight to the river, isn't it?" Mr. Shamblin asked.

I realized, then, what kind of drive they meant. The kind where you go visit the last place your son was alive. I said, "Yes, right to the river."

Mr. Shamblin firmed his lips, looked at his wife. "We were just on our way there." He paused, then said, "Have you been back yet?"

I shook my head. "We thought we'd wait a spell."

"You're welcome to come with us," Mrs. Shamblin said.

I read Caleb's sigh—just a wisp of a sigh—as saying he didn't want to. "We'll wait," I said. "You sure you all don't want to sit down?"

He looked at her, she looked at him, then he said, "Well, maybe we *could sit* a minute." He held the swing while she sat, then he eased down beside her. They was dressed real smart like they were going to another funeral, and sitting there on our swing, the paint peeling off, they made everything seem a little more dismal than it really was.

"What did you name your cats?" Mrs. Shamblin asked Misty.

"Callie and Boo-berry," Misty said, rolling her head the way little children do while locking their eyes on you.

"Blueberry? Is that because he's blue?"

"Boo-berry," Misty said again. "Like the ghost in the cereal."

"Oh, I see." Meryl's smile seemed sincere. "What grade are you in?"

"Third."

"That must mean Caleb is in the fourth—or fifth?"

"Fifth," Caleb said, jumping one of Misty's pieces and bringing Misty's attention back to the board.

Mrs. Shamblin asked them what were their favorite colors, what they liked to do, if they had bikes, this and that, and the children brought back short answers—like they knew something else was coming and this was just the preliminary act.

When there was a clearing in the Q and A, I offered, "Would you like something to drink?"

"No, no," Mr. Shamblin said. "Listen." He reached in his pocket, I thought, for a handkerchief or a mint. "We wanted to buy you a new roof—." He brought out a wad of money would choke a horse. I tried to remember did he run a roofing company.

"Or something," Mrs. Shamblin said. "We wanted to do something for you." I could tell she was used to cushioning for him.

Caleb lifted his eyes, kind of held them on a line between the checkerboard and the splayed cash in Mr. Shamblin's hand.

"It's kind of you," I said. "But we don't have any leaks. This roof's not that old."

"We want to do something," Mrs. Shamblin said again. "We want to help out."

"Help out?" I was searching.

"If Guy gave his life to save this boy, then this boy must be worth saving," Mr. Shamblin said, nodding toward Caleb. "We want to be part of it."

Caleb stared at the checkerboard. He had his fingers on a piece poised to slide forward to Misty's back row but was scanning for other moves he might have missed.

"You know," Mr. Shamblin said, gesturing widely across the yard, "we want to be involved."

"In Caleb's life," Mrs. Shamblin said. "And of course," she added, perhaps sensing the other pairs of ears listening, "that of his brother and sister."

Ron, I felt sorry for them. As a preacher's wife, I had seen the ways people shoulder grief. Losing someone, some folks tend to direct their energy toward someone else. Naturally, they might turn to the last connection their loved one had. In this case, it was Caleb. He'd been there. He'd seen their son die. I'd been there, too, but I wasn't the one trying to pump water from his chest.

Maybe they read in my face understanding and sensed softening on my part, for directly Clint Eastwood said, "If it's not too much of an imposition, we'd like you to consider our offer to send Caleb to a private school."

Imagine someone suggesting such a thing for Opie—and all that Andy Taylor would have felt! A wide splash of shock, for sure, like cold water in the face. But then mistrust and feeling looked down upon, then anger even, all rolled up like a rubber-band ball that bounced first one way, then another.

I had my mouth open to protest, but before I could, Meryl Streep held up her hand. "I know it sounds like a lot—*is* a lot to take in, Mrs. Kelly. But we'd really like to do something that would make a difference."

Caleb fidgeted in his chair, squinted at the checkerboard, tried hard not to look up. He was pretending not to have heard.

"I think he's pretty happy where he is," I said. "Aren't you, Caleb?"

He nodded, glanced quickly at me, I guess, to make sure I wasn't going to sell him out. "Yes, ma'am." Then to Mrs. Shamblin, "I'm happy where I am."

"Ah, happiness is fleeting," Mrs. Shamblin said. "Education—a good education—will be with you always."

"Just think about it," Mr. Shamblin said. "We don't want to push." He reached in his shirt pocket, took out a card, then reached it forward. Supposing he was handing it to me, I was in the motion of holding my hand out, but he lay it on the checkerboard in front of Caleb.

Caleb's eyes climbed slowly from the card to Mr. Shamblin, a testing glance. Then Caleb lowered his eyes, the way of a dog under its master's gaze.

"Just call if you need anything," Mr. Shamblin said. "Anything at all. As I understand it, you're the man of the family now."

When they left, they eased down the road, in the direction of the river—maybe looking back in their mirrors at our roof, or the windows, or something else on the property that might need attention. I tried to imagine the way they might see it. Certainly, Ron, it's not a big, two-story house like Opie lived in with Andy. Nor the double-decker where Howard and Marion Cunningham raised their children. It's just small and plain—faced with white cinderblock. By the same token, it's nothing like the shabby, ramshackle hut the Darlings lived in either.

But maybe they weren't looking back, the Shamblins, when they drove away. Maybe they were just slow approaching the place they were going to.

"That was a lot of money," Misty said. "I hope they don't get robbed."

The days of summer passed slower than usual. Dog days rolled in. The weeds along the road filled their tight parcels with colors that would signal fall, the deep purple of ironweed, the bright yellow of the buttercups. But the parcels held back, waiting. You could see the tips of the colors— but the blossoming, the rich fullness, was slow in coming. There wasn't a day went by I didn't think about mentioning the river, asking Caleb if he wanted to swim. But there was about him a brooding silence—like an electric fence strung round. You got too close and felt the energy from it—and feared its intensity—so you skulked around the perimeters. What, I asked God, was the right thing? Was it better to steer clear? Or should we go back to the river, try to salvage some of what we'd had before? Should I, for Caleb's sake, take him there, walk him through it all? Or should we let it lie sunken, hoping time and distance would erode it?

In the night hours, Caleb cried out, and I would find him asleep, clutching his tangled sheets tight around him. In the mornings, I'd ask about his dreams.

"I don't remember," he'd say, in a way that said he did.

He moved through his days like he was dreaming, too. He'd start off organizing his tackle box, then suddenly get up, leave the floats and lures and spoons in a jumble. He'd be patching the inner tube of Otcher's bicycle tire, then leave off, the patch unglued. Him and Otcher would set up their Tonka trucks to build a road, but Caleb would saunter away, leave the road a dead end. Him and Misty would be playing checkers, and he'd leave off in the middle. Would make her so mad, but she didn't quarrel. Maybe she sensed it would push him away further.

One day Caleb came in while I was mixing up my pie dough. "Is happiness really fleeting, Grandma?" he asked.

I saw then that the Shamblins had planted a seed. But I didn't know what kind of soil it had fallen to. I sprinkled more flour on my dough and mashed it in with my fork. Then I asked, "Do you know what 'fleeting' means?"

"Passing. Short-lived. Transitory." That showed he'd been in the dictionary.

Harmon's way was always to reference the Bible in the face of the dictionary, so I asked, "Do you remember the preacher in Ecclesiastes?"

"To everything there is a season," Caleb quoted, "and a time for every purpose."

"Do you remember what it was brought the preacher happiness?" I set out the clump of dough on the pie mat, commenced rolling it with the pin.

"Nothing," Caleb said. "He couldn't get enough of anything."

"Except?"

"To eat, drink, and enjoy the labor of his hands," Caleb said, pleased, I think, that he remembered so well. But you can see by this, Ron, how easily it comes to him.

Not knowing how to guide him to the rest, I just spelled it out. "And to remember your Creator in the days of your youth."

"But he tried everything," Caleb protested, "big houses, men singers and women singers, musical instruments—before he figured it out."

"Yes, it's true. He *tried* it all, then wrote about it so no one would have to go to all that trouble ever again." I lifted the edge of my crust, slid the glass pie dish under it, then began massaging the crust snug in the bottom with my fingertips, careful not to tear it. I glanced up at Caleb. He was watching my hands, but his look was far off. Finally, I said, "That's what got your daddy into trouble, you know. *Trying* everything."

"But he was trying things that were bad," Caleb said. "At least that's what the sheriff said."

I pinched the excess dough from the edge of the crust, put it in front of Caleb to mold. "Your daddy loves you very much. He just made some mistakes."

"I know." He kept his head down, rolling the dough between his hands. "Do you think you know when you're making a mistake, or it's only later you figure it out?"

"I'd imagine it depends sometimes. If your conscience bothers you at the time, that's a pretty good sign you're doing wrong."

Caleb didn't say anything, just squeezed and pressed the dough.

"What if your conscience says two things?"

I was afraid where he might be going, and then it just came to me, what Layne had said in his letter. I said, "But some things just happen—and they aren't anyone's fault. You can't blame yourself for something like Guy Shamblin's death. It was just his time to go."

The way he started, you'd thought I'd set off a firecracker. "I'd better go to the barn," he said. "I forgot to feed Boo-berry and Callie." He mashed his dough to the table and darted out before I could even say, "Go on then."

But I couldn't help replaying it, rolling it back and forth, as I flattened the next piecrust. How the thread of that day changed colors mid-spool, went from the gold and river green to the ash-gray face of Guy Shamblin, his gray torso, his gray-blue feet.

From the big rock upriver where we'd set up our picnic, I kept a pretty steady eye on Caleb with my binoculars. Though I couldn't see him in the shoals, I could pick out his orange swim trunks each time he waded back up along the edge of the sandbar to start again. I could observe, too, the young man and woman nearby, so I knew he wasn't alone. They paced back and forth across the sand, sometimes knelt at the edge of the water, sometimes moved from the sun to the shade of their tent. But there was no R-rated material, at least none that I could see. Still there was a familiarity about them, slight touches every now and then. It's clear now I should have been down on the sandbar, too—or kept Caleb out of the shoals.

You can show me at fault here, Ron. I know you can't portray any of us picture perfect. But listen, I was doing my best, three children in tow, one of them fairly intent on going his own way. I guess if we went on back, I could list times I wish I'd been there for Layne, too. But would any of those times made a difference?

When the girl started screaming, there was no mistaking trouble. It was of a hair-raising pitch. Misty, Otcher, and me, we turned that direction, then left the rock, started wading down the river. Though it was just knee-deep most places, the water slowed you down considerably, even flowing as it was the same direction we were going. And Otcher—it was to his waist, poor thing. I kept turning to make sure he didn't fall, but finally, I just picked him up and carried him. I prayed it was just a snake or muskrat that this woman—Meg Ryan—had seen and that Caleb wasn't in any real danger.

When we reached the shoals, we splashed up onto the sandbar, and I swung Otcher down mid-stride. The water from my shoes sloshed out, the sand slipped in. I ran past the tent to the other end where the woman stood. I can tell you, I was scanning the river the whole time for Caleb's orange trunks. That's when I knew the shoals were running higher than I thought, for there was too much movement to discern a swimmer, even close as I was.

My heart gave a sinking. "Where's Caleb? Where's my grandson?" I yelled.

"Guy's in the water," she said, pointing. At the time it sounded like she meant there were guys in the water—which I'd already figured out.

I told Misty and Otcher to stay put, then I waded in. The woman followed. We stayed near the bank, skirting the shoals. I could feel the tug of the current, but we weren't in the froth of it. You could stand—as long as you stood strong. We went on around the bend, and I saw the flash of orange of Caleb's trunks and this fellow's blue trunks way down at the river's edge, and I was thinking, at least they're both safe now, whatever's happened. But as we drew nearer, I saw Caleb pounding on the man's chest. How he learned to do that I never did find out. When we got there, the woman took over CPR, crying the whole time, "Oh, Guy, why'd you do it? Why? Oh, why? There was no reason," her voice trailed off in a slur. "You wake up now, Guy. Come back to me. Come back." She pushed on his chest while she yelled, and I saw her, more than once, wipe her eyes on her shoulder while she worked.

The rest is in the newspaper article, conveniently paper-clipped here for you:

Alum Creek Man Drowns, Saving Boy

Guy Shamblin, Jr., 22, of Alum Creek, drowned July 4 while saving a ten-year-old boy swimming in the Coal River. Paramedics pronounced him dead on the scene.

According to an unidentified woman at the scene, Shamblin jumped in to save a drowning boy, and after bringing the boy to safety was swept away in the current, which was running high after recent rains.

"He was a hero," the woman said, noting that Shamblin was as brave in death as in life. Shamblin was a U.S. Navy veteran.

The boy's name is not being released.

Curry Funeral Home, Alum Creek, is in charge of arrangements.

I never quite knew how the Shamblins got a hold of Caleb's name. Maybe it was the deputy. At any rate, not long after their first visit, they started stopping by regular-like. They usually brought some little something—a Frisbee, casserole, frozen steaks, some old pants and shirts of Guy Shamblin's they thought Caleb might grow into, Tinker-Toys, bubble-makers. Whenever I asked if they wanted Coke or water, they refused. They just sat on the porch and watched the children play. I guess maybe they needed a dose of children, none left to them now. To an extent, I identified. Losing a son to prison wasn't the same as losing one forever, but in the day-to-day of it, there were similarities. You couldn't pick up the phone to call. You didn't expect him pulling in your driveway. He wasn't around for holidays or birthdays—or for any gesture you wanted to make to him. He wasn't there for you to hug, the boy you'd loved so much since you first held him in your arms. In my case, though, I could at least write and receive letters—even if the prison mail took longer than you'd think, especially the jail being so close and in the same state.

Each time the Shamblins left, Mr. Shamblin—Clint—made a point of shaking Caleb's hand, looking him in the eye, and reinforcing, "If you need anything at all, anything, just give us a call."

The offer to send Caleb to a private school was still on the table. It hung like one of those paintings of naked people in the museum at Charleston, embarrassing to look at—though the museum folks themselves wanted you to admire it. The Shamblins asked me to notice it, and I looked, then glanced away. But one day on the porch, when they made reference to it, I managed to ask, "Did you send Guy to a private school?"

Clint Eastwood shook his head.

"We tried," Meryl said. "He just wouldn't stay. He wanted to be with his friends back in the public school."

"If we had it to do over—" Clint said.

Meryl patted his hand, "But we will never have it to do over."

Not long after that we got the call from *The Today Show*. And later, once we'd watched the program in its entirety, Caleb remarked, "They didn't even show the front of our house—after all the mowing I done—and the flowers you and Misty and Aunt Vera planted. Why was that?"

"Could be the back has more personality," I ventured. "It looks lived-in." Which was true. We had garlic strung up drying under the porch roof, and on the back wall, license plates from bygone vehicles—Harmon always tried to preserve them. We had an old couch where we sat in the evenings when the sun was too hot out front, plus an old freezer Layne had fixed, kept the venison we'd frozen after hunting season.

"But they showed the front of the Shamblin house," Caleb said. "And not their back."

He had me there. "Maybe their back isn't lived in," I said. "When you think about it, the place they live most is *our* front porch."

Just before school was about to start, Vera Lee told me she'd seen in the newspaper an announcement that the Shamblins were establishing a scholarship and donating ten thousand dollars to the science department at Guy Shamblin's high school—that is, the county school. There was to be a special tree dedication.

"Ten thousand dollars," Misty said. "Can we go?"

"You ought to," Vera Lee said. "Just support them. They've been through a lot."

"Come on, Grandma," Misty said. "We've never even been to the football field. At least, we can see what it'll be like before we have to go there."

"What are we going to do at a tree ceremony?" I said. "We'll feel out of place."

"Just show your respects," Vera Lee said. "That's what I would do."

And that's how we wound up at the edge of the high school parking lot. "Isn't it wonderful," the principal began, "that the memory and name of a hero like Guy Shamblin will live on? The students who might not have been able to afford college can now join their peers. Our science department will join the ranks of the best in the state, in the nation."

The Shamblins saw us, and when Misty waved, Mrs. Shamblin waved back. But they did not leave their post near the podium.

Some of Guy's former teachers and coaches were called upon to say how they remembered him. Then his science teacher, Mrs. Reed, was introduced. I remember there was at my feet a line of ants, and I was in the motion of stepping back to avoid their freeway when I heard a voice I'd heard before. "I think we will all always remember Guy Shamblin as a student who had the natural curiosity of a scientist," she began.

It was her voice first told me told me she was the young woman from the river—Meg Ryan. Then I recognized the sweetness in her face. Of course, she looked different—in clothes now and blown up as she was, pregnant, though not in a glaring way.

"He would have become a brilliant marine biologist," she went on, "and this gift from his parents is extraordinary. All our young scientists from Lincoln High will thank his parents for decades to come."

She didn't fog up any while she spoke—just kept the blinders on and focused on the speech before her. You wouldn't have thought she was anything more to Guy Shamblin than his teacher. But then at the end, she happened to glance up and see Caleb. There rose a deep blush in her face, and she stumbled over her last line. When she went back to the crowd, she stood beside a man—let's say, Kevin Bacon—who put his arm around her like a husband, not a father. I saw that Caleb's eyes followed, and when I looked over at the Shamblins, their eyes were fixed on Caleb.

They delivered new bicycles the next day. Then they started sending checks. Vera Lee said I had to cash them, would I want to insult the Shamblins? But I didn't, and the Shamblins called, insisting. Then they visited again. Still insisting.

"But you can't keep giving us things, Mr. Shamblin," I protested. "There's no reason for it. We may not have as much as you, but we're not poor."

"Now, now," Mr. Shamblin said. "We know this is what Guy would want."

"He was a good boy. He would want us to do this," Mrs. Shamblin said.

"We know we're doing the right thing," Mr. Shamblin said. "But are you doing right, withholding from the children what would make their lives better?"

I didn't know how to respond. You do your best, Ron, but when is your best not enough? When does your best fall short and turn to failure? Turn to a young man spending years in a jail cell? Eventually I gave in. At first, it seemed like we'd landed on the good side of the equation. The boy's life spared—plus extra money to maintain it. Then the strings began to show. They were thin as cobwebs at first. Mrs. Shamblin called to ask, Was Caleb getting enough to eat? What was it I cooked mainly? What all did I buy at the grocery store? Didn't we need more meat in the house? She hoped the children could have such and such, and such and such. Pineapples and star fruit was two of the things she named. Surely, they shouldn't be forced to eat so many sardines.

Now when I offered refreshment on their visits, the Shamblins accepted. Meryl followed me into the kitchen, looking things over. She didn't open drawers or cabinets, but just as soon as I got in the refrigerator, she twisted her neck to peer in.

One morning, not long after the Shamblins had taken the children to the circus in Charleston, I found Caleb in the yard stringing a long tow-rope from one sycamore to the other. All week the children had been juggling apples, swinging on grape vines, chasing the cats with chairs and belts. They had told me, big-eyed, they'd seen tigers and elephants and monkeys. Though the Shamblins had offered to take me, I hadn't gone. It was one less ticket to buy, one less thing to owe them—though as to that, I'd given up hope of repaying them for anything.

"You gonna walk that rope, Caleb?" I asked.

"Gonna try."

"Hadn't you better practice on the ground first?"

"Been practicing." He had the rope positioned about a foot from the ground, high enough to feel airborne, I figured, but low enough to avoid a broken arm.

"You ought to do that over the river," I said.

"You'd just like to see me get wet," he said.

"Maybe I would." For now we had commenced to mentioning it casually without the early heaviness.

"Caleb," I began. "There's something I've been meaning to ask."

"What is it, Grandma?" He kicked off his shoes, ran the bottom of his foot along the top of the rope, testing it.

"That day at the river, did you see anything unusual?" I watched his face, but he didn't look at me. He stepped up on the rope barefoot, grimacing as he wobbled first backward, then forward, then backward and finally, stepped back to the ground.

"Unusual?" he asked—almost to himself.

"Did you hear what they said, Guy Shamblin and Mrs. Reed? Did you see them—do anything," I faltered, "that concerned you, or bothered you?"

He walked over to the sycamore and held onto it while he stepped onto the rope again. He kept his hand on the tree, gaining balance.

"Because I worry," I said, "that maybe there was something going on that shouldn't have been."

"Like what, Grandma?"

I tested my thoughts the way you try the edges of an almond to find your sound tooth before chewing down. I decided to dial direct. "Maybe they were kissing," I said.

"It's no crime, is it, to kiss?" he asked. The rope stretched left then right with the swaying weight of him.

"Not with your husband or wife," I said, knowing full well I might unzip the memory of his mother and her boyfriend in the tree house. "But maybe with someone you're not married to—or not about to marry."

I couldn't tell if Caleb was considering this or just concentrating on the rope.

"Mrs. Reed gave you a funny look at the tree ceremony," I finally said. "Like you two were in on a secret together."

Caleb lifted his hand from the tree, held his arms out, and made a tentative step, grimacing as he did. He took a couple steps, the arches of his feet trying to curl around like bird claws. He jacked his arms up and down the way of chickens too young to fly.

"The Shamblins said—I might be—worth saving," Caleb punctuated each phrase with another shaky step across the rope. He struggled to stay up. I closed my eyes each time it looked like he would lose his balance and bobble off.

"Was you in such bad shape before?"

"Maybe it's God's way," Caleb said. He got back up on the rope, started again. "It's not hurting anybody—they've got the money—it makes them feel good—."

"It don't make *me* feel good," I said. "Whatever happened to 'blessed are the *poor*'?"

He was walking the rope pretty good now, moving with considerable more speed, which helped. When he reached the other sycamore, he held to it, turning himself around, never once stepping down. "*In spirit*," he said. "It's the poor *in spirit*. You can be poor in spirit, no matter how much money you have."

He had me there, trying to use Scripture to further my own ends. I watched him position himself again, his back to the tree.

"Caleb, did you see anything unusual between Guy Shamblin and Mrs. Reed?"

He stepped forward, his hand behind him still holding to the tree. "Grandma, I've seen you put stuff back on the shelf at the grocery store and known you wished for all the world you could keep it in your buggy."

"What stuff? Probably it was something I remembered we had already." I watched to see if this made an impression. "Did you hear me, Caleb? Something we already had." But Caleb kept his focus on the rope before him. He let loose of the tree and started back the other direction, his steps more assured than before.

I think of that day now and wish I could go back. I was close to asking if he'd made some kind of deal with Mr. Shamblin. I felt the words whirl in my head. But how did you ask a ten-year-old such a thing? Maybe I knew the answer and didn't want to tempt him to lie. But maybe I should have pressed. You like to protect their innocence, Ron, but Caleb will soon run out of innocence—if he hasn't already. He's launched himself off on a path, but what kind of path? Will he be able to backtrack if he needs to? Or is there some detour ahead we could steer him toward? I'm appealing to you because I can trust you—and because I know you're acquainted with solutions for impossible problems—like what we saw in *Apollo*. (I should admit here that I considered asking Spielberg for his help, but didn't know enough about his upbringing or his life as a young man. And like as not, he would want to throw in something supernatural—which doesn't really belong in a story like this—though I know you dabbled with that, too, in your series on the Cocoons.)

When the paramedics loaded Guy Shamblin in the ambulance, we still had hope. He didn't have a pulse, we heard them say. But didn't they have equipment to bring him back? Wouldn't they know how to save him? All evening we prayed—even little Otcher—but then come to find out the next morning, the answer was no.

But to get back to Caleb. About the time school started, the wildflowers alongside the road had finally opened. And I thought maybe we were back on track—just because the normal cycles had kicked in. It was a beautiful time—the skies blue and clear, the light vivid, the air with a crispness that showed fall was on its way, the days of summer ending. The children caught the bus in the morning. Caleb was occupied with homework. Otcher was home from Head Start in time for lunch. I had mornings to myself. Time to do the deep cleaning it's hard to do with children undertow. Mopping and washing the curtains, things like that. The Shamblins visited on the weekends, when the children were home.

One morning, when I was there alone, a man in a suit came knocking on the door. Picture him as Robert De Niro. He said he represented the Shamblins' insurance company and wanted to ask me a few questions. I invited him to sit on the porch. Then he pulled out a tape recorder. He termed it a routine visit, but, Ron, there was nothing routine in the questions he asked. Everyone, I guess, even the dead, has a day in court. On *earth*, I mean, and not just in heaven. Did Guy Shamblin seem like a man who might try to drown himself? Was there any reckless behavior on his part?

"Did he seem especially depressed on this day, Mrs. Kelly?"

"Of course, I couldn't tell," I said, "even with binoculars."

Did I know how much alcohol Guy Shamblin consumed before the accident? Did I know he had a record of mental illness since serving in the military? Did he have a death wish? Was there anything to suggest emotional distress? Did I think the current was strong enough to tow him under? Why didn't I try to save the boy myself? Did Guy Shamblin push me aside? What was his relationship with the unidentified woman in the newspaper? Did I know who she was? Had there been an argument of any kind?

I could see what he was after, and my mind divided itself. The Shamblins had been good to us—but they had set their hook in Caleb, too, and I'd been praying for a way of escape. Was this divine intervention? But how could I be sure the man—this Robert De Niro—wasn't baiting me with his own intentions. He must have sensed my doubt, for directly, he slid out a long sheet of paper from his briefcase. Had I seen the police report? At least, Caleb's testimony—what he had scrawled out for the deputy that day:

I was swimming in the long shoals and felt something take a hold of me. It was pulling me down. I fought to get free, then saw it was a man. I thought at first I was tangled in a drowned body but then saw it was the man from the sandbar. I felt him grab at me again, and I broke free, then pushed him away. The current carried us down to a little pool where the water was calmer. I climbed out, expecting him to follow. But he just washed on past. I ran along the bank, then waded in where I could, but he was floating face down. I couldn't get to him no sooner than I did. I pulled him out, and his girlfriend come along and started doing CPR. Grandma stayed a while, then went back up to check on Otcher and Misty. She tried to get me to go, too, but I waited for the ambulance.

I can see Caleb there—maybe you can, too—in his orange swim trunks, his wet hair pasted to his head, chill bumps along his arms and shoulders—because the sun was on its way down and the evening shadows falling. Probably his chin quivered as he spoke to the deputy. Most likely, he remembered all the deputies who'd come to the house before. Maybe he even recognized this one.

"Mrs. Kelly," the insurance man began. "If there's anything you can say that would cast a doubt on the *accidental* death of Guy Shamblin, you would spare us a case of insurance fraud, something that could lead to jail time if discovered later on."

I thought of what the Shamblins stood to gain—and then of how much they had lost. I didn't see how I could go against them and not go against Caleb, too. But I thought about the truth, how the truth is supposed to set you free. I did want Caleb freed, there's no doubt as to that. But there was nothing, except what I've written you, that I knew with certainty, and even then, Ron, it's not something I would swear to in court. It's all based, as Andy says sometimes on *Matlock*, on conjecture.

I held the police report damp in my hands. I stared at Caleb's handwriting. What had made Guy Shamblin take hold of him? What did Caleb mean about pushing him away? Did Caleb think, in the end, he was the cause of Guy Shamblin's death? And if he did, what did it mean that he was accepting the Shamblins' charity?

Finally I looked at the man. Square in the eye, I looked at him. "It was just Guy Shamblin's time to go," I said. "Just his time."

Ron, I'm writing you as a friend—not someone you know personally but someone who watched you grow up. The story—our story—is tricky in places. Not so cut-and-dried as people imagine. What's so far been reported is how one man's life was lost, but no one ever mentions the boy's life that was lost, too.

I cannot rue Caleb's success at the new private school where he's just been enrolled. Vera Lee says we just have to let nature run its course. But I have to ask, "Is it all for the good of the boy?" The Shamblins say Caleb stands a better chance of going to college—I can tell you he had no college aspirations before. But now he has begun writing what they call admission essays. The one he just completed—what I found in his room yesterday—is entitled "Saving Others." I can get you a copy if you think it will help in the filming.

The ending, Ron, is in your hands. You hold sway here—as much as anybody. Imagine how it was when you were fishing with Andy, and you suddenly caught a fish on a tangled line. How did you untangle the line without losing the fish?

Just remember there's going to be a young man watching, and he's the one most in need of a lifeline if ever anyone was. I know you'll be obligated to show other viewpoints, especially those of the Shamblins, maybe even Mrs. Reed's, if she will talk. I don't ask you to leave out their stories. Nor do I think ours is more important. All I ask is for equal playing time, that our story—our *loss*—be shown. When you meet Caleb, Ron, the spitting image of yourself a boy, I feel sure you'll want to save him, too.

—Your fan and supporter,
Mrs. Jewell Kelly

A WILD, TO THE RIM,

NET OR NOTHING,

OVEN-FIRED LADLING OF LOVE

No flash, no daring, no dash. That's what Grandmom said. Not the one scoring touchdowns or drag racing at the strip mine on Saturday nights. But the one sitting in the back corner, behind the scenes. The quiet, steady kind. That would be the boy you would want to marry, the boy to watch.

But I watched all the boys. Edgar with his bangs combed straight down to hide his startling green eyes; Perry with tousled hair like he'd just crawled out of bed; Nate with sleepy, droopy eyes like Rocky Balboa's; Colby with his downy sideburns; John with hair on his legs that grew thicker as your eyes moved up; Brent with a fine line of curly red hair down the middle of his abdomen to his waistband, maybe even past, you just didn't know. Buck with beautiful blue veins in his wrists that made the strap of his watch fit funny; Rod with the two halves of his chest carved nearly square—the way of my old Ken dolls; Jarrell with his Adam's apple that jogged when he talked; Archie with his tight, tight can, and the balance shifting from one side to the other when he veered left, then veered right, avoiding tackles down the field.

I watched for their shaven faces, the boyish faces of the ones weren't yet shaving, Old Spice, Mennen, Dial soap, their quizzical, glistening eyes, their fine taut arms in the motion of passing or receiving, the bulges in their uniforms which you couldn't help but notice. For all of them, for any one of them, for their curious parts and wholes, I was always on the lookout. But mostly, I kept my eyes on Seth, the coach's son, who had the queer taste of bubble gum and wintergreen Skoal whenever he kissed you, but about whom, my grandmother told me, there were rumors circulating.

"Boys like that think they've got something coming to them," she said, driving me home after the game.

"What rumors?" I asked.

"One minute you're kissing, the next, you don't know what you're doing—or what they're doing either." She made it sound like you could lose your mind and act like a maniac, something that certainly hadn't happened to me.

"I was just kissing him," I said, for the third time. "What's wrong with kissing?"

But it was awful to talk about—as if you were dissecting the soft belly of a small animal—awful to turn the skin back and poke. Why couldn't she leave it be? It was just what you did, what all the girls did. You cuddled with the players in the dark behind the locker room, leaning against the cold cinderblock wall, for just the few minutes before your parents—or in my case, grandmother—rounded you up and carted you home.

I always wanted to say, "Be glad I'm not like Lorraine or Chrissie," but I didn't want to tip her off.

In the dark, I sneaked a glance and tried to read her expression by the pale green light of the dashboard. Her eyes were intent on the road. We drove in silence. Then I couldn't stand it. "What rumors?" I asked again.

"Never mind, Phoebe. Enough for you to know there's evidence against him."

I imagined her on the phone with Lorraine's mother, making lists of Seth's misdemeanors, the way they usually did, pooling their clues, deciding why one boy or another wasn't good enough. As far as I was concerned, he was innocent till proven guilty. And what could he be guilty of? Had he been with another girl? Not Amanda Kirby, surely. He'd sworn he didn't like her. But even if he did, would I, could I, through sheer focus and will, have *liked* him—*loved* him—any less?

"Just ask him where he was last weekend," Grandmom said, "when you wanted him to come sample your pumpkin pie."

"He was at his aunt Regina's house in Boone County."

"Yes, but who did he have with him?"

It wasn't like Grandmom to invent trouble where no trouble was. But I couldn't tell whether she believed everything other people said, or if she kept her own counsel. My mother had always remarked how hard it was to slip something by Grandmom, but I suspected her senses were dulled with age. It was easy, for instance, to talk on the phone with one person but say I was talking to another.

When we got home, Grandmom turned on the TV and poured herself a neat bourbon. Rupp Arena slowly materialized on the screen, and along with it, her beloved band of Kentucky Wildcats jogging backwards on the basketball court.

"Don't go to bed yet," she said, seeing me turn down the hallway. "Stay up and watch the game. There's a new guard, name of Kyle Macy." She sat with her legs folded under her in the recliner, her scissors and newspapers beside her on the table. It was her habit to cut out coupons, box scores, little newspaper articles for her files, but when Kentucky was on, she gave the team her full attention.

"I'm tired. I just want to go to sleep," I told her. Mostly I wanted to be alone so I could roll over in my mind how the evening had been, how the whole season had been.

In my bed, I started it post-game, imagining the boys in the locker room, showering, the water glistening on their skin. I'd seen pictures in magazines at Chrissie's house of players in the showers, their Loch Nesses loose and parading. I was sure our own players didn't dawdle like these, though, taking time to wash their ankles, for instance, or contorting themselves to wash their backs in a spirit of ease and leisure. For one thing, our boys slipped out the back of the locker room even before the lights were shut off over the field—like they'd run through the showers car-wash style—just enough to smell soapy. The ones who didn't have girls trickled out the front of the building slowly, then stood with the parents who were waiting for sons, looking for daughters. I'd come to think of those boys as the front line, blocking everyone else from the action behind the line of scrimmage. But like linemen, they could not block out everyone and left gaps that I came to think of as a kind of protection.

The boys were never more lovely than after a game, no matter if they'd won or lost. It was different, of course, either way. If they'd lost, they were sullen and pitiful, all their enthusiasm gone out, blaming themselves and each other, blaming the coach, blaming you. And you'd think of things to console them, like cradling their warm necks with your hand, combing your fingers through their wet hair—just some slight touch—and then gradually they'd slough off their disappointment, like snakes shucking off old skin. If they'd won, as they'd done on this night, they showed themselves proud, cocky, strutting, and against you, would press hard and harder—as if they were still in the game, intent on showing who was boss. On these nights they had more daring, and you had to distract them, tame them, or you'd wind up having to rub their Nessies.

Lying there, I thought of the way Seth kissed me, the sweet salt of his lips, the inside of his mouth warm against the chill of late November. He had slipped me a sliver of peppermint—like a hot secret passed between us—that had set my heart to rocking. I don't mind saying I lived for moments like that—all that swirling you felt. He was inside my coat—for I'd worn a coat big enough to go around both of us. While we kissed, I felt his hands move behind to cup me, and I slid my hands around to hold his rear end, too. I anchored my hands in the tight corners of his blue jean pockets and pulled him to me. It seemed to satisfy him, being against me like that, and I rested in his arms.

Some girls went further, I knew, even with so little time, and it seemed like they didn't mind it. In the darkness I could hear a zipper, the rustle of fabrics, a kind of panting. "Mmmmm," someone said.

"Mmmm," I said, quietly, in my bedroom to see how it would sound.

I could still feel Seth against me. I hugged my pillow tighter, and eventually, after some time, went to sleep like that.

"If you can't pass the ball," Coach Lewis yelled, "then dribble it." As if that would be any better.

I bounced the ball and crab-walked backwards, using my body to shield the ball from Archie. Now and then, I felt Archie's hand on my back, then on my behind. I felt his thigh brush up against mine. I kept backing into him. Then I felt him take hold of my waistband. That was illegal, I knew, but you could get away with it if the coach wasn't looking. Easily, Archie could have darted around, stolen the ball, and gone to score at the other end, but he let me keep dribbling, backing into him. From time to time he swatted at the ball to make it look like he was trying.

I kept my eye on the ball so it wouldn't bounce off my shoes—but Archie's hands were a distraction. I felt them quick yet gentle—like falling leaves glancing off you.

When there was no place to back, when I was nearly under the basket, I stopped dribbling and looked for someone to pass to. Finding no one, I mustered the courage to shoot. Archie stood tall, arms vertical.

"Just an easy kiss off the backboard," the coach yelled. Why did he call it a kiss?

I closed my eyes and heaved the ball from my shoulder, lobbed it over Archie's fingertips. Opening my eyes, I saw the ball bounce on the rim. I prayed for a friendly bounce—just one single friendly bounce. The ball did bounce and bounced again, wobbled, rolled around the top of the rim, leaned in, leaned out, then dipped over—and finally rolled out.

"That's okay. Good try." Coach Tackett said it in a tone you might use with children. Coach Lewis blew the whistle, and Lorraine ran in to replace me.

Grandmom sat in the bleachers, but I didn't meet her eye. Instead, I went and stood beside Seth, who'd gotten himself sidelined for too much fouling.

"What was that about, Phoebe?" Seth asked.

"What?"

"You know what."

"What?"

He glared. His ears were red the way they got when he was angry. "You out there with Archie, that's what."

"What about it?"

"What were you doing?"

"Just playing," I said.

"Yeah, right. *Playing.*" He wheeled around and headed for the door.

I swallowed hard, watching him, then blinked a few times to ease the burn in my eyes. I gave a side-glance to the bleachers to make sure Grandmom was absorbed in scrimmage; then I took off down the sideline after him. There was a lot of maintenance to keeping a guy once you got him.

Outside, there was no sign of Seth, and in my T-shirt and shorts, I felt the sting of the December air. The door to the furnace room was unlocked, so I peeked in and sure enough found Seth sitting on the concrete ledge, leaning against one of the units. He was staring straight ahead—he didn't even look toward the door. The room was even colder than outside, but I stepped in anyway and eased the door shut.

"What's wrong? What're you so sore about?" My voice cracked as I went to him. I touched his shoulder, hoping to soothe him.

He pulled back, folded his arms. "You know what."

I didn't say anything, just stood there, feeling the chill deepening.

"How can you say you're serious about me if you're flirting with every other guy who comes along?"

"That's crazy. You know how I feel about you."

"You think I don't see?"

"But, Seth, I love you."

"How do I know that?"

"Because I tell you all the time!"

"Then show me."

"Show you how?"

He reached for my hands, then pulled me toward him. I looked back at the door. The furnace room didn't have any windows.

"Kiss me," he said, smiling and pulling me near.

"Somebody'll come," I said. But I knew Grandmom's tendency to lose track of time once she got involved in practice.

"So?"

I leaned in and kissed him, and he pulled me between his legs. Maybe it was the shock of the warmth of his bare legs against my bare legs, maybe the difference between stiff denim jeans and the soft polyester fabric of gym shorts, but I felt a fast heat come to my face when I kissed him. The taste of his bubblegum and wintergreen washed over me. The scent and taste swirled through our kissing. But then I felt his hand sliding up under my shorts, and I took a step back.

"Someone'll come," I said, trying to stay him with my eyes.

"So?" he said, reaching for my hand and leading it to his waistband. "Here."

It seemed like all roads were bound to lead below the horizon. He pulled my hand in farther, farther and farther until my fingers brushed his Nessie under what I guessed was a jockstrap. He groaned and pushed into my hand. My face burned.

"I can't. Grandmom will come," I whispered.

"Grandmom, flandmom," he said. "Hang your grandmom."

He cupped my rear end and pulled me snug against him, leaving my hand inside his shorts. I nuzzled my head in his chest. He smelled of deodorant and sweat, laundry detergent, and of himself, just Seth. I loved him, didn't I? He was breathing hard, like panting. It was like an over-friendly dog, insistent on being rubbed, always nudging your hand even when you were ready to stop. Sometimes you just wanted the dog to lie there, wait for you to make up your mind to give it attention. You wanted to meet it on your own terms.

I slid my hand from his waistband around to the small of his back and massaged there in a spot I knew he liked.

But he pushed me away suddenly. "You can count on this," he said, standing. "I won't beg." He tore off toward the door, but over his shoulder yelled, "Maybe you'd rather I send Archie in!"

"The trouble with you," Grandmom said, on the way home, "is you don't know how to do a layup. It's fundamental. I can't believe one of the coaches hasn't taught you. Why don't you get Seth to teach you?"

The tears bunched in my eyes. "Seth thinks I like Archie."

"You and Archie *seem* awfully cozy. At least you let him guard you close."

"*Let* him? How am I supposed to stop him?"

"Throw an elbow." She glanced over, nodded her head, more serious than I'd imagined. "That'll make him keep his hands off."

I guess I wanted his hands off, but I wasn't sure. I couldn't imagine throwing an elbow into his sweet, chiseled face, or his washboard ribs, for that matter. I didn't want to hurt him. It was easier to imagine nuzzling against him as I'd nuzzled against Seth in the furnace room. Each time you started with a new one, you got all the sweet buildup, and you could go awhile, if you went slow enough, without getting backed into a corner. Somehow with Seth, things had gone fast. Maybe I'd been used to dating the ones who didn't expect as much, didn't expect anything, and so were delighted with whatever there was.

That night when I thought of Seth, I replayed how warm it was to be against him, skin to skin, how good it always was to kiss him. Lying in the darkness, I felt my face heat up, the thought of my fingers around his neck. I hated myself for touching him, and I hated the way dogs could wear you down, wear you down until they got all the attention. At the same time, I hated myself for not doing more. Seth, after all, might turn out to be the *one*, the first. When my friends talked about it, they were always relieved to be done with it—like it'd been some yoke they were glad to get shed of. Lorraine had planned it all out, made Danny tote a sleeping bag. It was about as romantic as you could dream of, under the stars, the bed of his truck, out at the cemetery, the radio playing. When your friends told you, you didn't pass judgment. You wanted the details, without seeming to. The trick was to show enough interest to keep them talking, but not so much they'd think you were a virgin.

But Seth didn't call, and didn't, and didn't. Not that night, nor the next, nor the next. A week went by, him avoiding me at school, returning my notes unopened through the vent slots of my locker. It was like being tossed around in a rock tumbler, fractured, chipped, bruised, heaved round again. Where had it gone wrong? Was it just in the furnace room? The rest had been good, hadn't it? Cuddling together nights after games, holding hands in the hallway, sharing lunch, kissing on the bus, both of us hunched so low the driver couldn't see—though the window beside us steamed. Had I really been flirting with Archie on the court? Did I like him? I loved watching him walk, his wild swagger. Did he like me? Should I send out some feelers to Lorraine to find out?

"Don't you have a book to finish this weekend?" Grandmom said, catching me on the way to my room with a bag of pretzels.

"I haven't even started."

"If you start tonight, you can make a good dent."

I rolled my eyes. "No one does their homework on Friday night, Grandmom."

Her eyes brightened. "Then you can watch the game—*that's* what lots of people do on Friday nights."

When I moved in with Grandmom, I had known there'd be adjustments. I just hadn't known Kentucky would be one of them. Not that I had anything against Kentucky—or against anything Grandmom took a fancy to. It was natural she would have her interests, and I would have mine. And it was sweet, really, the way she cared for her Wildcats. She'd grown up in Lexington, her father a Kentucky fan, and he'd raised her that way. At some point, she married a West Virginia man, my granddaddy, and moved with him to Huntington. He died early, even before I was born. She had loved him, she always told me, heart and soul. Sometimes, I had in mind to ask her, what part was *heart*? What part *soul*?

In the family, she had the reputation of being a little kooky—someone who preferred flea markets to the Diamond department store, horse racing to NASCAR, *National Geographic* to *Good Housekeeping*. But her great passion—second to Kentucky basketball—was preserving endangered species. She spent hours writing letters to congressmen and senators, even presidents of other countries, urging them to save leopards, alligators, kangaroos. To the Kentucky governor, she pleaded particularly for the cave shrimp, piping plover, and pearly mussel.

When I first moved in, I had thought it was poachers she was after, but Grandmom said it was the less obvious intrusions—like strip mining and dam building, timbering and spraying pesticides—that were most threatening. She fretted about natural habitats where there had been no human contact but now suddenly was. In almost every case, she said, human contact brought disaster. In the bathroom she'd pinned up a poster, a Virginia big-eared bat hanging upside down that said, "Stay out of my hair, I'll stay out of yours." Until I got used to it, it scared the daylights out of me in the mornings.

Not that I cared. I much preferred a house wallpapered with bats and crocodiles to the shenanigans at either parent's house. My mother's boyfriend had had the habit of hugging me too often and too tight. And my father's new wife blamed me for every piddly thing gone wrong—plus wanted me 24/7 to babysit her two spoiled toddlers, both still in diapers. My parents had batted me back and forth until I didn't know whether I was coming or going. They both outwardly expressed regret that I'd come to live with Grandmom—maybe they were afraid I'd turn out loopy, too—but I think deep down they were glad to start fresh without me. Besides, I didn't see that Grandmom was any crazier than anybody else once you spent regular time with her.

On this night, she had popped herself some popcorn and sat with what she called a neat bourbon, untouched—waiting for tip-off.

With my book, I took a seat at the far end of the couch, furthest from the TV. I figured once I got deep enough in, thoughts of Seth and Archie and Lorraine and the pitiful, silent, lifeless phone would fade to background. So thinking, I tied my hopes to Pip, who was in trouble, turned upside down by a villain. I followed him home, where he had to tiptoe round things, stealing bread, dodging his older sister's darts. I stayed with him, right at his heels, shivered with him, fretted with him. Then the crowds roared. It was Rupp Arena, and I had to fight to dig back into the pages. Pip stirred the Christmas pudding. He learned about escaped convicts but went ahead and stole a file from his brother-in-law. He was dreadful under the sway of the man from the marsh. The crowd at Rupp Arena tried to drown out Pip on his errand. Glancing up, I saw Grandmom on the edge of her chair, gripping her armrests.

"Jack's open," she yelled. "Right under the basket."

I willed myself to stay with Pip and accompanied him, pork pie and all, back to the cemetery. The convict ate like an animal but treated Pip more kindly than before. Pip went home, worried about the pie. Then, just as he was fleeing the house, his heart burdened with guilt, the king's soldiers met him at the door, pointing their muskets at him. A solemn quiet entered the room—the absence of the crowd's roar. I surfaced momentarily to hear the solitary drumming of the basketball on the floor. Then I heard a swish. I can honestly say it was the sound of the ball rushing through the net that made me look up. The camera zoomed in on the white uniform of No. 4, a sweet-faced player, with wonderfully dark eyes. He dried his hands on his socks. Bounced the ball three times. Eyed the basket over the ball, then shot again. The ball made such a patient, graceful arch you could tell by its trajectory it would go in, even before its descent. It wasn't just a swish but was more the sound of the ball slapping the bottom of the net. It started as a *thread* then ended quickly, a snap, like *-et*, to sound like *threat*.

"That's the new guy," Grandmom said. "Kyle Macy."

Through the years stacked between that one and this, I don't remember whether Kentucky won or lost. I don't remember who they played. What I remember is that *threat* sound—those nothing-but-net shots of

Kyle Macy from the foul line. Everything else fell away. Pip and his haranguing sister. The convict of the marshes. The room. Seth. The silent phone. Grandmom. The crowd at Rupp Arena. There was a gentle nudging in my heart—the way of a dog cracking the door open with his nose—and instead of shutting the door, I left it open, and through the crevice, I watched Kyle Macy.

I left my finger on the page of the book, pretending to read, but my eyes kept darting back to the TV and to Kyle Macy dribbling the ball, passing, and shooting. He had a spell on the ball and sent it where he willed. No one I knew handled the ball like that—not Jarrell, not Brent, nor Archie, certainly not Seth. The ball was a yo-yo attached to his hand and he did tricks with it. It went out from him, then came back. He pushed, pushed, pushed it, and all the while, it kept coming back. There was something thrilling in it—like the first time you saw a trapeze artist let go of one swing to fly to another. It had about it that kind of breathless dazzle.

When I went to sleep that night, I dreamed of Kyle Macy. He was running and shoving the basketball. He pointed with his free hand, directing traffic. In my dream, I was on the court. But he didn't point to me, didn't look at me. Still, I had the feeling the ball was coming my way. It was such an intense feeling that when I woke, my heart was racing, and I had to lie there, reassuring myself it was only a dream.

But that didn't stop me from feeling it all day, that peculiar fear of the ball coming to me. What would I do? Who would I pass to? But then at the boys' practice, when the ball did come, I managed to send it off to Jarrell without having to bounce it.

"Good pass," Coach Tackett said.

Once, off to the side, I bounced one of the extra balls, trying to yo-yo it like Kyle Macy. It was harder than it looked. Seeing me, Coach Lewis said, "Not with your palm. But your fingertips. That way you have more control."

The whole practice, Seth didn't give me a glance, and I kept my distance. A wedge had entered, and each day's silence drove it deeper until the gap was so wide, it couldn't be bridged with ease. Archie sensed this—anyone with a finger on the string of the web work at school could sense it. He hovered closer than before. More than casual brushes now, his hands lingered. There was a solidity in the way he touched me, kept his hand on my behind. I thought maybe he did like me. I thought maybe he would ask me out.

But one evening in the locker room after practice, Stella said, "I wish Archie'd keep his hands to himself."

"Tell me about it," Darlene said.

The heat rushed to my face. Had they all been watching?

"What'd he do?" Lorraine asked.

"Felt me up when I went in for the layup." Stella cupped one of her breasts.

"Roughing the passer," Molly said.

"That's what they're there for, girls," Chrissy said.

"Not mine," Stella said. "I wish I had a way to protect them."

"You need a better bra," Lorraine said. "We all need better bras. Somebody ought to invent one. I jiggle all over the place."

"I just wrap this bandage around and around," Darlene said, unraveling herself like a spool of thread. "It works. You should try it."

"That wouldn't stop Archie," Stella said.

"No," Chrissie said. "Nothing stops Archie."

"They make straps to hold the guys in place," Darlene said.

"Oh, yeah," Chrissie said. "Good thing."

Some of the girls snickered.

I stuffed my sneakers in my duffle bag. "You could throw an elbow at Archie," I said, and for once, I wished I'd taken Grandmom's advice.

"Listen to Phoebe. Is that the way you handled Seth?"

"Maybe a knee would be better," Denise said.

"What happened between you and Seth?" Chrissy asked. "I thought he really liked you."

"Oh, I don't know." I calculated. "I guess he likes other girls besides."

"Who?" Lorraine asked.

"Who?" some of the others asked. Their attention turned to me in a way it usually didn't.

I shook my head. "I'm not one to spread rumors. It'll come out." I gauged to see if one of them flinched, but if someone did, I couldn't tell it.

———

Christmas was a sad time, I don't mind saying, to be without a boyfriend. I missed Seth—more than I might have missed him if I'd been at school, with other people around. But it was the holiday break, and I was home with Grandmom. I missed his voice, the warmth of his hands, the strong grip of his fingers, the slow winks he gave, the way his muscles—in his arms, in his thighs—felt under my hands when I clutched and rubbed him. I missed the hair on his forearms, his fluttering eyelids when he closed his eyes to kiss. The scent and taste of wintergreen and bubblegum mixed.

But what was the point of mistletoe or eggnog without a boyfriend? Of trading gifts when you didn't have someone special to give to and receive from? What was the point of caroling in the dark, of hot chocolate afterwards, of putting up and decorating a tree? You just had to hang back, go through the motions, try not to ruin everyone else's holiday.

But there were evenings when I'd shut my door and lock it quietly, then fold myself on the bed, my tears sogging my bedspread. The ache started deep inside—maybe there where my heart was—then radiated out to the tips of my fingers and to the tips of every part of me. I wanted and wanted and couldn't have told you for all the world what exactly I wanted. Yet it wrung me, on spin cycle. It was dreadful to be under the pull of such strong currents. I thought of Pip and the villain's power over him, driving him to steal files and pork pies. And what villain was it gripped me? Seth? Archie? Or something else all together? And what did I feel driven to do? At times, I'd be bursting with energy, wanting to tear through the world like the Tasmanian Devil, spinning and spinning my destruction, caught up in the whirlwind of it. But at other times I just felt quiet, wanting only to be held and comforted. And so I cried, under the radar of Grandmom, and then dried my eyes and tried, in her presence, to put on a good face so she wouldn't send me back to live with either of my parents.

"This is the proving ground for Kentucky," Grandmom said, pointing to the Notre Dame players just out on the court. "They haven't played a team this good yet."

It was New Year's Eve, and everyone else had gone to Lorraine's bonfire. I had turned down the invitation so as not to be the only one without a date. Grandmom had volunteered to accompany me, as usual—having now taught herself to record games on the TV. But who, after all, wanted to be seen all the time with her grandmother?

"You want me to leave this bright light on so you can read?" Grandmom asked.

"I left my book in my room."

"It's just as well," Grandmom said. "You might get tomato sauce all over it."

She was baking a homemade pizza for halftime. There was no reason, she said, why we shouldn't celebrate like everybody else on New Year's Eve.

Of course, she had every reason to celebrate. Her Wildcats were on TV, for one thing. But beyond that, she had told me, there had been strides writing legislation to save a whole slew of endangered species. To top it off, one of her contacts had sent her a big photo of himself and a companion holding a baby brown pelican rescued from an oil spill. For Grandmom, all was well with the world—or at least moving in that direction. And as far as she could tell, everything was fine with me, too.

"He's just a sophomore," Grandmom said. "Look how he holds his own with all those juniors and seniors. It's because of his composure."

Kyle Macy did seem to bring a calm to the game. The announcer said he had ice in his veins, and while this didn't sound like a good thing, it was said as a compliment. Kyle didn't force the pass or shot either one. I didn't see how anybody could be so patient with the ball—or operate with such faith that things would eventually work out. But most of the time, things did. One of his teammates got free, or an opponent fell off balance, and there was an open shot to take.

There were nine other players on the court, but Kyle made it his game. Still, though he played every quarter, he wasn't a big scorer. He didn't hog the ball. He spent a lot of time feeding it to the forwards under the basket. For loose balls, he scrambled. He had a ruggedness you couldn't help being drawn to. His thighs were lean and muscular. That was in the day when players wore real shorts, not the baggy pajamas you see them in now. He had rounded muscles everywhere, but he didn't look like the Hulk or anything. In fact, compared to a lot of the other players, he looked small, though the announcer said he was six-foot-three.

Sometimes when he went to the foul line, the camera would train in, and you could see his deep, dark eyes under his full, dark eyebrows, peering over the rounded edge of the basketball like two black onyx stones rising up over the rim of the earth. He was something to see.

Back then, I imagine I wasn't the only one watching him. He was probably every coach's dream player, dribbling down the court, stopping suddenly and popping straight up like a jack-in-the-box. He'd shoot—talk about poetry—and the ball would arch through the air and—*t-h-r-e-a-t*—slap the bottom of the net on its way through.

"I believe they ought to give him more than two points for those long shots," Grandmom said. "It takes a lot of practice to do that. Not everyone can, you know."

"You should write and tell somebody. Get the rules changed."

"Maybe I should."

At halftime, with Kentucky leading, Grandmom brought out the pizza on a TV tray and set it down between us. It had about everything you could imagine—or want—pepperoni, sausage, mushrooms, green and black olives, pepper rings, red and green bell peppers, onions, a couple different kinds of cheeses. You'd have thought she'd been stocking up for such an occasion.

She slid two of the cheesiest slices onto a plate. "I've got another little surprise in the oven," she said, handing the plate to me. "Don't let me forget."

Though I didn't say, already I had caught the scent of her oatmeal cookies.

The cheese on the pizza was hot and stringy and looped down to my chin when I took my first bite. The hot tomato sauce burnt my skin, and I wiped my mouth quickly and just as quickly leaned in for a second bite.

Grandmom settled back in her chair with a paper plate in her lap and took her first bite. "Mmmm," she said. "We ought to do this more often."

"It's really good," I said. "Better than marshmallows and wieners."

"Well, they have their place, but this *is* better if I do have to say so."

Later when I loosened a third piece and dragged it over to my plate, Grandmom said, "I've been thinking, Phoebe. The coaches ought to let you play more in practice."

"Why?"

She shrugged. "You could improve that way."

"They don't care if we improve. We're just warm bodies—for when too many of the guys are out hunting."

I heard they're thinking of starting a team for girls next year."

"Maybe," I said, seeing then where she was headed. "But that would be for girls like Stella and Denise—the ones who can really play."

"You could play—if you had more practice."

I squenched up my face and frowned.

"I mean it." She reached for the pizza and worked loose another piece for herself.

"I know, Grandmom, but you must have missed something."

She was in the motion of taking a bite, but she stopped midair and looked at me.

I hurried and tried to soften it. "I'm sure last practice you probably saw me score for the other team."

"And that was a very good shot," she said, reclining back again as if I'd given more evidence for her side. "Just be glad you scored. Jenny Woodrum didn't score a point for anybody. You've got good height and speed. Those are the main things to start with." She nodded her head, took a bite, then rested her pizza in her plate while she chewed.

I was left trying to puzzle it out. The winter months gave her basketball fever, no doubt about that. But I knew she turned to horse racing in the spring. Would she want me to train as a jockey?

Just as the players lined up center court for the second half, Grandmom leapt from her seat. At first, I thought she was helping with the tipoff, but then, watching her dash for the kitchen, I caught the first scent of burn. I got there in time to see smoke pouring from the oven.

"Go open the back door," she said, stuffing her hands into oven mitts.

I held the door, and she ran out into the cold night, down the porch steps—quick and surefooted. She dropped the pan of smoking cookies in the snow.

"Mercy!" Grandmom said. "How's that for a bang-up New Year's Eve! We almost had our own bonfire!" She was laughing as she came back up the steps. But then in the light of the doorway, I saw her eyes rimming with water, and her nose red. "But I wanted it to be something you'd remember."

The look on her face made me want to cry, but I fought and didn't. In the next minute she was laughing again, her wet eyes sparkling. She said, "But I guess maybe now you *will* remember it. Ha-Ha."

That's when the smoke detector started squealing. We went around opening windows and setting up a cross-breeze with a fan. The air that rushed in was cold. It was really cold.

When we finally got back to the TV, Kentucky had fallen behind. As bad as Grandmom felt about the burnt cookies, you could tell she felt worse about the score.

"Come on, Phoebe," she said, patting the couch. "They need us."

We both sat on the edge of our seats, and through the ticking seconds, I felt my nerves straining. The lead went back and forth. But Kyle Macy stayed cool as the leader of the pack. The clock ran lower and lower, but when the ball came to him, he still welcomed it like an old friend.

"He's a good one in the clutch," Grandmom said. "You can't rattle him."

The house grew colder by the minute, and while we needed to close the windows, we couldn't leave Kyle Macy. Every time he took the outside shot, our hearts soared with the ball. Every time he went to the foul line, we planted our best hopes with him on that line. Slowly, the scoreboard tipped and stayed tipped in Kentucky's favor. In the end, we won. Probably the house was freezing by then, but we were too fired up to know it.

That January, a big snow came—a big, two-foot snow. It caught a lot of people off guard, and it took days and weeks to clear the roads. The further out you lived, the longer it took them to get to you. We were snowed in for a couple of weeks. The school buses couldn't run, leaving me homebound and restless. Through it all, Grandmom and I watched Kentucky. Most of the time, she fixed popcorn. And while she sipped her bourbon, I drank ginger ale—splashed with cherry juice to dress it up.

Gradually it came out, how she had played basketball in high school. "That was back when you divided your team into offense and defense," she explained. "Some girls stayed on one end of the court, some on the other. I guess they thought it was too much to ask the girls to run full court."

"It's pretty far, Grandmom. Especially when you have to run back and forth, over and over, the whole game. I don't know how they do it—without more subs."

"Look at these fellas," she said, pointing to the Wildcats. "They're not even out of breath. It's because they've trained their bodies. Back when I played, they thought a girl would mess up her female parts if she ran too much."

"Mess them up? How?"

"Just the jarring, I guess. The *exertion* is how they put it."

"Then what would happen?"

"Nothing," she said, taking a sip of bourbon. "Nothing would happen. They were wrong."

Sometimes the Kentucky games would be recorded and broadcast late at night when there was no other planned programming. On the evening news, the sports announcer would warn you the score was coming so you could, if you wanted, hold your ears and run into the kitchen to miss it. I guess Grandmom thought I was a convert. And maybe I was, but she didn't push. Every now and then, what she'd say was, "Now that was a textbook layup."

I had to admit sometimes I could see the beauty of the thing—like a ballet move the ice skaters made—a smooth leap with a graceful arm-lift that in this case happened to deliver a basketball *softly*—I could see now why the coach called it a *kiss*—off the backboard. Some small part of me wanted to try it. And I have to tell you, this was new. For though I'd been staying for basketball practice before the holidays, it was just an excuse to spend time with Seth and Archie and the other guys. I had never thought of myself as a player.

For a while, thinking about it was as far as I got. The snow kept everyone in. There was no school. There was no basketball practice. I slumped around from room to room. Grandmom probably got tired of hearing me sigh, tired of my long phone calls with Lorraine, where we compared scorecards, why Jarrell was hot, why David and Kenneth were not. Neither of us mentioned Seth anymore. I was trying to move on, and I guess Lorraine didn't want to open old wounds. A time or two, I started to mention Kyle Macy, but for some reason I didn't.

One day just as I got off the phone, Grandmom came to my room with a big box. "Look what came in the mail for you."

Inside, there was a deflated basketball. I turned it over and over in my hands, tracing my fingers over the Spalding.

"I had to save twenty box tops to get it," Grandmom said. "I had to choose between saving cows or rubber trees. But in the end I got the one I thought would last the longest." She clapped her hands together. You would have thought it was her basketball.

"Once the snow melts, you can take it to the court down at the elementary school. But for now, you can dribble in the basement, just to get a feel for it."

"It's cold down there."

Grandmom frowned. "Not that cold."

True enough, it wasn't *that* cold. I wore long johns under sweatpants, as she instructed. She got out the bicycle pump and put air in it for me. All I wanted was to dribble without looking at the ball. How did you get it to behave like a well-trained dog, or a yo-yo, going where you told it, as if it were on an invisible leash? I bounced the ball with my fingertips, as the coach had instructed. At first, I just walked around, my eyes to the ceiling while I dribbled. The ball bounced off my shoes more times than it didn't.

When the snows finally melted, I took the ball to the court at the elementary school and eventually got to where I could run the length of the court without looking at the ball and without losing it. I imagined Kyle nodding his head, clapping. Grandmom asked, didn't I get lonely practicing by myself? It was peaceful, I said—and it was. I didn't tell her Kyle kept me company—though I guess maybe it wouldn't have surprised her.

Beside the court there was a series of brick posts where once a wood fence had been strung. You could bounce the ball off one of the posts, and it would come back to you like a pass. I practiced getting the ball to ricochet from a post to meet me further down the court. I can't say how many loose balls I chased across the playground all the times I underthrew or overthrew the posts. But gradually it got to where I could run the whole court, passing to the brick posts—imagining it was Kyle running alongside me, passing the ball to me. Back and forth we'd go till we were under the basket.

That's where confusion and disappointment set in. I would throw the ball up any which way—off the backboard or just on top of the rim—hoping it would fall in. On TV, Kyle made it look easy. But it took a lot of strength, just getting it there. When I couldn't luck it in, I would throw it hard, trying to force it off the backboard or lodge it in the rim so it wouldn't pop back out. But it popped out more often than it fell through. I do not say I didn't think of Seth all this time. Or of Archie. Or of Jarrell. But I kept them at a distance. Their minds were already turning to baseball practice—which, till that year, would have been the place I wanted to be. From time to time, I thought about what Grandmom had said, that some people believed too much running would ruin your female parts. Maybe my parts were wilting, I thought, and that explained why I didn't care so much about sitting in the bleachers watching the boys.

When we shot, I talked to Kyle about the boys I knew—because Kyle and me, we could be just teammates, just friends. "Kyle," I would say. "I have a problem."

"What is it, Phoebe?" he'd say.

"I heard that Lorraine likes Seth."

"That's okay, isn't it? You're over him now, aren't you?"

"I guess. But I wonder who started it?"

"They're both free agents, right?"

"Yes, but what if it started before we broke up?"

"Don't let it get you down," Kyle would say. "You've got other things going on."

In secret places in my notebooks, I took to writing Kyle's name and No. 4. I clipped box scores and newspaper photos and put them inside my locker. There were photos of Jack Givens and Coach Joe Hall, and, of course, Kyle Macy. When I opened the locker, Kyle was there, his brow fierce in concentration, encouraging me to stay composed no matter what kind of day I was having.

One day Chrissie stopped at my locker. "Wow. Who's that?"

"Just one of the players from Kentucky," I said.

"Is he professional or college?"

"College."

"Do you know him?"

I shook my head. "I've just seen him on TV."

"No wonder you stopped hanging out with our boys. How long have you liked him?"

"It's not like that," I said, shutting my locker.

And it wasn't. Well, it was, but it wasn't. How could it be? Although he was the person I thought about all the time, it wasn't in the same way I'd thought about other guys before him. I could talk to him in ways I couldn't with regular boys—mostly because he listened and didn't hog attention.

By early spring, Kentucky was on the road to a national championship. Every game—Florida State, Miami-Ohio—there was more at stake. And Kyle was there every game, pulling it off at the foul line. Or feeding it to Jack or Rick Robey under the basket. There was a beauty in the games themselves, the way the players moved down the court like a herd of gazelles. My grandmother and I spent whole quarters standing in the middle of the floor, intent on every pass, every shot. Sometimes we clung to each other, hid our faces in the other's shoulder so as not to see. But in the end we found ourselves jumping up and down like it was as much our game, our victory, as theirs.

In the Mideast regional against Michigan State, everyone thought Kyle would meet his match against Earvin Johnson—a guard the announcers called "Magic." But all that showdown proved was that there was no one more magic than Kyle Macy. Down through the final stretch of the game, he scored enough from outside and on the foul line to give Kentucky the win that propelled them into the Final Four.

While the games heated up, so did my practices. All day at school, it would build in me. I felt a fullness, like little bolts of energy firing in my legs and in arms. My fingers grew restless, anxious for the first brush with the ball. Then after school, once I had the ball, my heart beat giddily on the walk down to the court.

There, I dribbled, and the first bounces of the ball sent a message to the basket—that I was coming, that I was on my way. No longer was it about forcing the ball but now was more about coaxing it. I understood better its rhythms and tendencies and adjusted myself accordingly. I tell you, I kept a dizzying pace. Round and round, I went, backwards and forwards, spinning first one way, then another, throwing would-be defenders off balance, moving closer and closer to the goal. Everything else fell away—papers I was writing for English, Seth and Lorraine holding hands, all the newspaper clips of whales and wolves Grandmom was trying to save.

I worked on my jump shots, setting up garbage cans in the middle of the court and learning to shoot from behind them without falling forward and knocking them over. Envisioning myself a rocket, I sprang straight up and only when I peaked, perfectly vertical, would I release the ball, launching it—arching it, ever so gently—toward the goal. The follow-through was key. My eyes, my hands stayed with the ball even as it left me. At such times, I felt connected with the net. I would send out the ball, and the net would welcome it, embracing it once it entered the rim. The net would hold it momentarily, swaying back and forth, then let it drop softly to the ground.

So close were we in those moments, I didn't know where I ended and the basket began. We were tangled up together, the basket, the ball, and me. Winding around and around in the zone, I lost myself, shooting and rebounding and shooting again, full throttle, all in a heady circle of give and take. An hour or two later, I was utterly spent. And when it was ended, I was panting, my legs aquiver, my face hot as an oven. I would go back to the house, and Grandmom would say, "Goodness. You better get a drink of cold water." In those evenings, my heart was light and happy.

The layup alone remained elusive. I would lie awake trying to negotiate its intricate movements. In my mind, I replayed Kyle's layups, or Jack's, and my own miserable attempts at it.

One evening home from shooting, I admitted it flat out. "I still can't do a layup, Grandmom."

"It's got to be one fluid motion," she said, "like you're taking a running jump to touch the backboard, but on the way up, you drop off the ball."

"I know. But you have to dribble till you jump, then catch the ball while you're jumping. Then lift it up, nearly one-handed," I said. "Kyle makes it look easy."

"He's been at it a long time, I expect. You know when he was in diapers, his folks had him dropping the ball in a basket."

The next evening, sporting a pink sweat suit, Grandmom accompanied me to the playground. She jogged in place on the court. Then moved somewhere else and jogged. It was such an unusual sight I had to turn my head to keep from laughing. I tried to imagine her a young girl in uniform.

"It's been a long time since I had my hands on a basketball. I probably can't even dribble."

"Here," I said, catching her attention, then bounce-passing it. "See if you can."

She wrinkled up her mouth and squinted her eyes and pushed the ball down, then caught it with both hands. Down again and up and caught. Down and up and caught. Then she sent it down, and patted it down, and patted it down again, without catching, and there she was, dribbling. "It'll come back," she said, watching the ball as she dribbled. Back to me she passed it. Solid.

"Now, let's work on the layup," she said. "Show me what you can do."

I started at half court and dribbled at a slow jog. When I got to the basket, I managed to catch the ball and jump at the same time. Then I hoisted the ball from my hip and felt it slip from my fingers. It spun out into the playground, and I chased away after it.

When I got back, Grandmom said, "You're doing much better at not looking at it. That's the main thing."

"What am I supposed to do after I jump?"

"Let's see." She went to half-court and bounced the ball, revving up. For half a minute, I expected her to break into a run like Kyle Macy. But instead, she walked, bouncing the ball, turning the problem over in her mind. When she got near the basket, she seemed to ladle up the ball—it reminded me of ladling anyhow—and sent the ball upwards. It hit the bottom of the rim and came back down fast—so fast I had to run over and knock it away to keep it from hitting her in the head.

"Goodness," she said. "It's faster than it used to be." She was laughing, so I laughed, too.

"Anyway, Phoebe, I think you need to scoop up the ball with one hand, and use your other to protect it from the top or side—so no one can strip it from you. The Kentucky players have football dummies standing in their way when they go up for a layup—so they have to concentrate and hold the ball tight. When you've got it good and balanced, pull the top hand away and lift the ball up with one hand. Just tap it into that little square—like you're tossing a rock at a window you don't want to break."

She went back to half-court and tried again. This time she brought more energy and skipped a little off the ground. She made the same ladling motion with her arm, going up, and she delivered the ball off the backboard into the basket.

"Wow," I said. "You really can play."

She winked at me. "It's coming back. It's in the blood, you know."

Over and over, I tried to ladle it as she'd done. Sometimes she'd say, "You jumped too late," or "You jumped too soon." Or she'd caution, "Don't put it up so hard—just lay it up easy." We practiced it that day, then the next, then the next.

Eventually, I felt in my body the shape of the layup emerging. I dribbled, caught the ball, got my right hand under it like a ladle and scooped it up. Then my left hand assisted to keep it from spilling. When the ball was balanced on the tips of my fingers, I pulled my left hand away, and made a faint springing motion with my right hand. The ball rose toward the backboard.

I did it over and over. The mastering of it was gradual, culminating in days with more hits than misses—though still a fair share of misses.

"You've got it," Grandmom said. "Once it gets in you, your body will remember it forever."

The layup was the single riskiest thing I learned in basketball. For while it brought you closer to the basket, it also put you in danger. You opened yourself up and made your body vulnerable. You couldn't jump backwards because you were jumping forward, flinging your body through space. You charged into it full steam, and once airborne, your body extended outwards. You surrendered control. I thought of all the players I'd seen on the floor after an opponent had taken their feet out from under them. On TV, the guys ended up in the crowds, on top of cameramen even! For me, it took a courage I'd never had before. But admittedly, too, there was a certain freedom in flying yourself at such a speed—and in knowing you could make the landing.

The satisfaction was tremendous. While the jump shot brought connection with the basket, the layup brought a different kind of communion. It was the difference between *sending* the shot from far out and *being* the shot from deep within. Time after time, I would move in, straining, reaching. Even more than with the jump shot, I felt a part of myself go upwards with it. And then I lifted the ball as something of an offering to the basket. It got to be where I was rewarded most of the time with the kiss off the backboard and the swoosh of the ball down through the net.

Kentucky won the national championship that year. For me, it was a bittersweet victory—meaning an end to a season that in no small way had sustained me. A famine would follow, I knew, and it would be a long time before the first game of the next season.

But one day that summer, just after I came in sweaty from the court, Grandmom looked up from behind the newspaper she was reading. "Guess who's coming to Huntington on Saturday?"

The smile on her face told me.

"Kyle Macy?" I said, my eyes stretching wide.

"He's signing autographs at the Ford dealership."

All week I lost sleep. Over and over, I played it in my mind. Would he recognize me as a kindred spirit? Would there be a court where we could play? Would he maybe give me his jersey—like you saw athletes do on Coca-Cola commercials?

The line for autographs was about twenty people deep when Grandmom and I pulled in the parking lot. Immediately we were beset by car salesmen, but Grandmom waved them off. "We're not here for cars," she said. "We just came for Kyle."

In line were old and young fans alike and quite a few girls my age standing with their mothers. I don't mind saying I felt a tinge of jealousy. But I thought, too, if someone put all of us on the court at once, I could hold my own against any of them. I don't know if that's true or not, but I had a brief, momentary surge of confidence.

While we stood there, I fingered the paper that had my questions on it. They were pretty specific—about the backwards layup, the behind-the-back pass, occasional moves I'd seen Kyle pull off—not in the least showboating, Grandmom had said, but only when necessity called for it. Occasionally, Kyle stretched, looked back in the line, probably wondering how many more times he'd have to sign his name. Each time he looked, I tried to build my courage to look back, but always my strength failed me.

Every now and then Grandmom stepped from the line to get a better view of him. I knew she was anxious to ask him how recruitment was going. And there was a part of me, I guess, hoped she would brag to him. I could just hear her saying, "You should see Phoebe do a layup." This would be the only way, I figured, for me to earn his respect.

Finally, with just one person in front of us, my heart pounded like it would shatter my ribcage. I held the basketball under one arm so my sweaty hands wouldn't dampen it and create a smudge where Kyle was going to sign his name. Finally, when the body standing between us moved away, and I found myself face-to-face with him, all my thoughts turned to mush. I couldn't think of the first question. He smiled at me, and I smiled back. At that moment, I knew that was as far as I could take it. It had been silly to think of asking him any questions at all.

Grandmom lifted the basketball out from under my arm and placed it on the table in front of him. "Hello, Mr. Macy. I'm glad we finally got to meet you. We were up all hours watching you play. We followed every game. My granddaughter Phoebe here is your biggest fan. I think she wants to marry you."

It took me a minute to understand what she had said, and when I did, my face flashed even hotter. It was such a shock—even from my Grandmom.

Kyle must have registered the surprise on my face. What had been a friendly smile now broadened to a full grin that pulled his dark eyes into it.

I was too surprised to say anything at all.

Suddenly, he moved around the corner of the table with my basketball in his hands and dropped to his knees. From there, he took my hand, and placed it on the basketball.

"Will you marry me?" He was still grinning, and it occurred to me he was trying to turn it all into a joke between him and me—to show my grandmother. But it only made me blush more. I felt the silence in the room where before there had been busy chatter. I felt everyone's eyes on me. A camera flashed. Then flashed again. From somewhere, a photographer had emerged.

I took a deep breath and let it out slow—just as if I'd been about to shoot a free throw, then I said, smiling, "I'm sorry, Kyle Macy. It's not like that."

I met his deep-set eyes over the basketball, long enough for him to realize—and for me to realize, too—that it really *was*. All he'd expressed on the court—playing his heart out every game—had made an impression on me, and I'd expressed it back—even without him there to know it. We'd felt the same aches—driving to connect with the basket, straining to move closer to the rim, flinging ourselves in the air toward that goal.

We'd felt the same exhilaration, the same pleasure when the basketball swayed snug in the net, or when it threaded through, then dropped back down to fill our hands anew. There was love in it for sure, no one could deny it, a wild, to the rim, net or nothing, oven-fired ladling of love.

The next day there was a picture of the proposal in the newspaper—him on his knees, holding the basketball between us. Had I been the newspaper editor, it's the picture I would have chosen, too—far more dramatic than a regular signature shot. But my favorite photo—of the handful the photographer mailed us—is the one I keep framed on the wall now. Not Kyle Macy proposing or even dribbling in front of me, motioning for me to steal from him, or the one where I'm dribbling and he's defending, but it's the one where we're posing: him standing between me and Grandmom, all three of us resting our hands on the basketball, and she's sneaking a glance over at me, so much certain joy in her eyes.

It was funny, really. For a long time, before his daughter married, Russell was afraid she would turn up pregnant. He braced for it each time Marlie came back to visit, especially when she'd gone a long time without seeing them. Pregnancy out of wedlock wasn't so uncommon as it used to be, and it seemed like it could happen to anyone. One man he knew had three daughters who came back that way. Each time it happened, Russell felt sorry for him. At least he and Evelyn had avoided that kind of scandal. But now whenever he saw the man in the yard on his riding mower, a young boy in his lap driving, Russell felt behind his sternum a hollow place.

This time, when Marlie said she needed to see them, Russell had hoped it was to tell them she was pregnant. That way he'd at least be able to spend time with a grandchild before he died. Or maybe, knowing a grandchild was on its way, something inside him would fight to stick around longer to watch the little one grow up. He'd always had a lot of love, but now, as he caught sight of the finish line, he felt he had even more—and couldn't help wishing for someone new with whom to share it. But when Marlie had swung down out of her jeep a few days ago, there was no bulge under her blue-jean jacket, and no pregnant woman would have worked as she had done since she'd been home—unless she was trying to lose a baby.

Now from the window of his bedroom, he watched her splitting wood.

She was making the maul work for her. It was different than with his son, Frank, who had big shoulders and arms and could bully his way through the wood. Marlie held the maul at the tip of the handle and swung with a long, high arch and with such a light touch that Russell worried the maul would fly out of her hands and injure her—or some innocent bystander. Her rhythm was consistent, even machinelike. Clomp. Pause. Clomp. Pause. Clomp. Clomp. Pause. They were clean splits, too. Right through the heartwood. None of that splintering of the edges he had no patience for. Had he taught her to chop like that, or had it come by instinct?

When she was down to nine or ten logs in the oak pile, Russell left the window and went to the closet for his jacket.

"See if you can get her to stop after this," Evelyn said.

He shrugged. "I don't think I can stop her. She must be working through something."

Clomp. Pause. Clomp. Pause. Clomp. Clomp. By the sound of the split logs falling on the ground and on top of each other—like the high-pitched scattering of bowling pins—he could tell the oak was well seasoned.

He went back to the window. What did the neighbors think, driving by, seeing her doing his chores? By now they'd probably heard. A quadruple bypass, not wholly successful. He'd been given lists of instructions on everything from eating to avoiding stress to doing gentle warm-ups and stretching before loving his wife. And the kicker: enjoy your life because you might go at any time. Which, when you thought about it, was really the truth for everyone. But hearing the doctor say it brought it out from whatever drawer you'd been storing it in and made you turn it over in the light.

"Alan hasn't called the whole time she's been here," Evelyn said. "I guess they're not talking again." She was leaning over the bed, lining up old photos of the children, different rows for each decade.

"Maybe they just need a vacation now and then," Russell said.

"We never needed a vacation." Evelyn straightened up, put her hands on her hips, and arched her body backwards till it took the shape of a strung bow.

Russell crossed the room and gently commenced rubbing her shoulders. "Maybe you ought to work on the kitchen table," he said. "You wouldn't have to bend over so far." He felt her muscles loosen under his fingers.

She leaned back into him. "There's just more room here," she said. "I've been meaning for years to get these in albums."

There were gray pictures of the baby years, some lightly touched with paint. Then came the fading colors of the toddler years when Kodak must have been working out a new chemical formula. All the early photos had white borders with scalloped edges. In the next row, a group of orange-tinted photos showed the kids in junior high with braces and big glasses and their hair parted straight. Finally, there was a set of momentous occasions—proms, graduations, and most recently, though already five years past, Marlie's wedding. The special haze of the formal shots blurred Marlie and Frank through their adolescence and early years of adulthood. Off to the side, Evelyn had piled a few Christmas photos taken since the wedding, but these seemed more an appendix. Of what was to come, there was little trace.

"She'll work herself to death," Evelyn said. "Didn't you see how tired she looked?"

He put his arms around her, and they stood together, the whole lengths of their bodies touching. Russell took comfort in it.

"I thought she looked okay," Russell said, but he knew what Evelyn meant. There was some new worry etched in Marlie—she wore it on her face and carried it in the line of her stance. He couldn't quite pinpoint it, but he'd noticed it the evening before in the kitchen when she was stuffing peppers and cabbage rolls with ground turkey—all healthy for his heart, she told him.

"She's a good cook," Russell said, remembering, too, the mashed turnips seasoned with cinnamon and nutmeg.

"And a good eater," Evelyn said, easing from his embrace and bending over the photos.

"And eater," Russell agreed.

But who wouldn't eat a lot after all the work she'd done? Since coming home, Marlie had cleaned the gutters and chimney, raked the yard, bagged the leaves, even dug a drainage ditch out at the side of the yard where water had been collecting. Russell had seen her eyeing the sun-cracked cedar siding on the northeast wall of the house and knew she was thinking of replacing it. She had never been one to sit still. He supposed that was what kept her out of trouble. Frank had sown his oats, but Marlie had been a model daughter, what people called All-American, with good grades, after-school jobs, a stint as pitcher on the softball team, volunteer work at the nursing home and Habitat for Humanity.

Evelyn pulled a photo from the deck and placed it at the end of one of the rows. It was of Marlie and Frank on a camping trip. They had on their fishing vests, and their faces were rosy from sunburn. It'd been decades since Russell had seen smiles as big as that.

"I'll see what I can do," he said.

He called Josie the dog, and together, they went out. The sour scent of sap and drying leaves hit him, along with the hint of wood smoke from somebody's chimney. Russell took a deep breath and savored. It put him in mind of other autumns, other years, when he was out doing the things Marlie was doing. Clomp, pause, clomp. The splitting went on. Down through the yard he strolled, pausing to examine the large trunks of maples he'd planted when the kids were small. Their old wounds, from when the children had tried to tap maple syrup, were healed now, and the trees looked healthy with only a smattering of red leaves left in their bare tops. The trees would probably outlast him. But the day would come when they, too, would lose their strength, maybe rot from the inside out, or succumb to disease.

He steered himself again the way toward the barn, toward Marlie. By now she would have seen him in the yard. He was giving her time to collect herself, if anything needed collecting. At the barrel incinerator, he stopped again, peering in to make sure the last of the letters had burned completely. He'd lately taken to some housekeeping that involved rereading and destroying letters he and Evelyn had sent when he was in the Navy. It brought back their early years and plied his nostalgia for young love. But he didn't want anyone else—not even the children—reading them. There'd been a romantic side to him he wasn't keen on sharing with anyone but the one who'd inspired it. He and Evelyn had talked it over first. They were having conversations they wouldn't have had three months ago before his surgery.

The clomping and pausing at the woodpile drew him on, but still he did not hurry. He gazed curiously in the little creek, studying a spark plug and a piece of old plate—might have been his grandmother's—what all the recent rain had uncovered, odds and ends just thrown away, no use to anyone now. Josie stayed with him, both of them circling and doubling, like hounds that couldn't puzzle out the scent of the trail.

When he finally got to Marlie, she had finished the pile of oak but was getting ready to start in on the hickory.

"That old tree was back there on the corner of the property a couple of years," he said. "I hated to see it go to waste. I wouldn't have bothered if it'd been poplar."

"I know," she said. "On account of the popping."

He nodded, then threaded his way through the strewn logs to one of the unsawed tree trunks he and Frank had dragged from the woods at the end of summer. That was the week of his heart attack. "Why don't you rest a spell?" Russell suggested, sitting back on the log. "You've been working since you got here."

Marlie's eyes and nose were red—and Russell understood she would start splitting the hickory to hide that she'd been crying. He marveled at the mix of softness and ruggedness in her. When the children were little and got hurt, they came crying to you, and you knew to put on salve and a Band-Aid to make it better. But when they were older, they hid their tears. And who could begin to know how to mend their wounds if they suddenly chose to reveal them?

But he was running out of time. That's what the doctor had said. And it was funny and absurd. Because he didn't feel bad. Nothing hurt him. He felt tired, but that was all. And anyone, at seventy, could feel tired. He felt fine really. He had been strong through the surgery and recovery. So far, nothing had been able to sink him. But then, none of it had done the trick to repair him either. He supposed it was how people in coastal areas felt when a hurricane approached. That there was some dark treachery lying in wait beyond the clear, blue horizon was just about more than you could believe.

Josie looked up at him, wagging her tail. He picked up a stick and threw it deep in the yard for her. She bolted. Marlie watched her.

"She won't overdo it, will she?"

"Nah," Russell said. "It's been two weeks since she had her stitches out. Dogs, they just get back up, go back to themselves. It's people who take a while to bounce back."

With her boot, Marlie shoved over one of the hickory logs, then bent over and rolled it a few feet toward the short walnut stump where they did their chopping.

"I wish I could help," Russell said.

"I can get it." She commenced rolling it again and wrestled it up, end over end, onto the chopping block. Not once did she have to take its full weight.

She wiped her forehead and stood back, eyeing the log and gathering her strength. In her short hair and on the sleeves of her flannel shirt—one of his that Evelyn had put in the rag pile—Marlie was sprinkled with sawdust and wood chips.

Josie came back dragging the stick. Russell took it and held it, watching her and trying to gauge her need for rest. She sat down and looked up at him, wagging her tail. She was a mix of collie and retriever, and maybe some other breeds, too, that hadn't yet manifested.

Marlie stood resting with the heel of her hand on the maul handle as though leaning on a cane. She was more angular than he remembered, and it seemed to him that since she'd married, she had toughened up. The word *hardened* came to mind, but he didn't like thinking marriage would do that to you. Still he could tell she probably went to the gym a lot.

"You work like this at your house?" he asked.

"I wish," she said. "I wish there was woods—and firewood to bring in—and a fireplace."

"You all could move back here," he said. "Plenty of room to build. Whatever piece of the property you wanted."

He watched her face, but she pulled up the shoulder of her shirt to wipe her forehead. It was funny to him, that either one of them could slice straight through a log, but when it came to speech, they were blocked up as a beagle that had swallowed a sock. On TV, people talked. Everyone talked naturally about everything. He didn't see how it was possible in real life. If you had the script before you, that'd be another thing.

"Pretty day for chopping wood," he said. "Not too hot."

"No," she said. "Nor too cold either." She had rolled up her flannel sleeves, leaving only her long-john sleeves to keep her wrists warm.

He tried again. "You think Alan would ever move back here?"

Again, she wiped her forehead—but maybe it was her eyes, he couldn't tell. "I don't know. He might."

"Does he help around the house?"

"Some."

"He probably wishes you would sit still."

"I try to stay busy."

"I was busy my whole life," Russell said, wagging the stick at Josie. "Now I wonder if it would have gone slower if I hadn't been so busy." Josie rose and faced him, fanning the air with her tail. He swung hard, sent the stick to the edge of the woods. Josie ran fast, so fast that when she got near the stick, her rear end seemed to overtake her front end when she tried to stop. She nearly went over in a somersault.

Russell grinned and looked at Marlie. She was grinning, too, and when she met his gaze, he sent his love, and she, perhaps feeling its intensity, ducked and shied away. She stepped up to the chopping block, then lifted the maul to let it rest on top the log as a batter might do before swinging. Then she stepped back and lifted the maul high and brought it down hard. The maul bounced back up as if it were a rubber hammer—and she caught and managed it from far back on the handle.

"Whoa," she said. "I wasn't expecting that."

"Good thing you didn't get hit in the head. Hickory's hard, you know. This tree was gnarled besides. You might have to use the wedges."

Marlie sized up the log. "I'll give it another try first." His daughter had a determination that Evelyn likened to his own. But what was strength in a man, he reasoned, might be viewed as stubbornness in a woman.

Marlie squinted her eyes at the top of the log, then gave the log a half turn as if a new angle might make all the difference.

"Your mother thinks you're working through something." He tried to dive in without thinking. "Is anything wrong?"

Marlie lifted the maul over her head, then brought it down considerably harder. The maul went deep, deep into the log and stuck there.

She pried up and down, but the maul was lodged tight. Russell scanned the ground for the wedges, and when he saw them, went over and picked them up. The weight of the tiny irons was startlingly heavy. He brushed the sawdust off and carried them to her. It gave him a chance to inspect the log.

"That dark wood in the middle, the heartwood," he said, pointing, "is dead, you know."

"Well, it's all dead now."

"I mean even when the tree's living, the dark part is dead—or dying."

"Funny they would call it heartwood then—and not deadwood," she said.

Russell smiled. "It's the sapwood, the white part, that lives. The outside part. I saw a TV show on it last week. But the heartwood—what's dead—weathers better than anything. It's full of tannin that makes it resilient, for outdoor furniture and things like that."

Sensing her interest, Russell continued. "I know you know about the rings?"

"Summer and winter?" she said.

"If I'm not mistaken, they said *spring* and summer. But anyway, it's the same thing. Fast growth as opposed to slow. The bark's a big deal. It's more important than I ever realized."

She nodded. "All the nourishment?"

"Yep. Water and minerals move up through it."

Marlie nodded. It was easy to talk about trees and animals—any natural occurrence. That was what they listened for, out in the world, to tell each other. It was just difficult for either of them to say a soft thing to each other.

"Probably you ought to lay the log on its side," Russell said, "and pound the wedges in that way."

She rolled the log to the ground, positioning it on its side. The maul handle jutted straight up. Then she inserted the first wedge, and with the sledgehammer, pounded it in as far as it would go. She tried prying the maul loose, but still it wouldn't budge.

Russell moved back to his place on the tree trunk, out of her way, and took the stick from Josie. "This is the last time," he said. "Then you'll have to rest." He threw the stick hard, and as he did, he felt a tightness in his chest where his stitches had been. The stick went up, end over end, and whizzed over the barn to the other side. Josie followed it with her eyes, half-jogging, half-dancing the same direction. Russell expected it would take her a few minutes to understand where the stick had gone.

Marlie pounded the second wedge twice, three times, then four, and freed the maul and the first wedge. She turned the log upright again and split it in half, careful not to hit the second wedge, which fell out as the wood separated. Then she turned one of the half logs back up on its end, took up the maul again.

"Well?" he said.

"Well, what?" she said.

"What's wrong? Is there trouble in paradise?"

"I guess there's trouble in paradise," she said, lifting the maul high behind her and bringing it down to split the half into quarter pieces.

He steadied himself to prepare for the possibilities. Whatever it was, it might hurt him. Divorce would hurt him. But he would try not to take it too hard. He couldn't afford to. There was his own heart to protect now, his own life at stake.

"Are you dying?" he asked. Because to him, this seemed a yardstick now by which everything else could be measured.

"No," she said. "*I'm* not. But the marriage is. Alan and I have separated."

There. It was out. Now they could deal with it. It wasn't so bad as a terminal illness, he told himself. He would still have his daughter. But there was no guarantee in that either. Sometimes, with trouble in a marriage—at least on TV—depression seeped in. Then there was always suicide to worry about.

"I know how you feel about divorce," Marlie said. She swung high again, then guided the maul deep into the new log, where it stuck. She turned the log on its side, inserted a wedge near the maul. "But that's what we're going to do." She didn't look at him, just reached for the sledgehammer and started pounding the wedge. The ringing echoed off the hills around them.

Josie came back marching with the stick, pleased to have found it. She held her head high so the stick wouldn't drag the ground—giving the impression of a dog swimming. When he reached down, she brought it right to his hand, obedient in every step. The stick was slimy where she'd been chewing.

To Marlie, he wanted to say, "It's your life." But he held back, knowing she would take it as the jab he meant it to be. There were new rules now. You tried not to say things that would be hurtful—in case it was the last thing you wound up saying. You didn't leave anyone on bad terms. You didn't walk away harboring guilt or hatred or anger. You finished everything like it was the last time, like there would be no other chance. In case there wasn't.

The maul was free again, and he watched her lift it, saw her steady herself. Her eyes scanned for the invisible vein she would aim for.

She sliced all the way through, quartering another half. It had the note of finality to it.

"Nothing can be done to fix it?" Russell posited.

"No."

She gathered up the quarter logs and loaded them onto the trailer behind the tractor. Then she wrestled another log up to the chopping block. She was moving from the smallest logs to the largest—the top of the tree down—and was still in the knotty region where the limbs had been.

"I'm sorry," she said. "I know it's not what you wanted."

It was old-fashioned, what he felt about marriage. But there were things he knew—how you learned the blueprint of someone, how they learned the blueprint of you, what it was to open the doors, walk through each other's rooms, the lovely pleasant ones but the grief-filled ones, too. And even the ones where the other person was too scared to tread alone. How a person could suddenly go around shutting all those doors to someone you'd opened them to, he didn't know. And then there were people who would open the house to lots of people, lots of lovers. How easy it must be, he imagined, to say the wrong person's name in a moment of honesty, just the way they did on TV shows. Or you might think you were waking up beside one person when it was really another. He thought of the divorced people he knew. The world was changing. Not much stayed constant. Divorce these days was more the norm than fullterm marriage. Even if you lived in a place where there was a semblance of constancy, the TV might give you other ideas.

"Well," he said, feeling it his turn to speak and wanting to say a true thing, "I'm sorry it's not working out."

She went on clomping and pausing, clomping and pausing, every now and then ringing the wedges with the sledgehammer. He envied her, for he knew how it felt to work like that. He knew the heft of the maul, the back stretched to near breaking, the scrunched abdomen, the way your hands were jarred with every blow—the way that jarring vibrated in every part of you. Marlie struck so hard sometimes her feet came off the ground. It was hard for him to sit still and watch her. He was used to sparing Frank whenever he needed it. And vice versa. That was the way to keep fatigue at bay.

Out in the woods he heard Ray Stoddard's hounds howling and running, probably on the trail of a rabbit. Josie heard them, too, and stood up. She looked from the woods to him, back to the woods and back to him, expectantly. Easy to read.

He was about to say, "Go on," but then remembered her recent incision and the brush and briars she would be apt to tear through in the woods. "You better *stay*," he said.

She barked, as if in protest. Then she lay down, he thought, pouting. She kept her ears up, though, monitoring the turns, coming and going, near and far, in the woods.

Marlie chopped. He wondered if he and Evelyn had done something wrong, somehow created a restless daughter. After college, she'd been one of those who couldn't find her niche. Couldn't, for some reason, take hold, though she was good at most things she attempted. Before settling down with Alan, she'd moved from job to job, state to state. A man like that was called a drifter. A woman was just called flighty.

Josie lifted her nose in the air like she was scenting out the rabbit the hounds were chasing. Russell reached down, patted her head. "It's for your own good," he said. But he hated making her stay when what she wanted was to run with the other dogs.

"We're not in love," Marlie said, between swings. "I guess we never were."

"Love," Russell said. It was not something he talked about—though he thought about it probably more than most would expect. He'd been, he supposed, one of the lucky ones.

Marlie rested, holding the maul diagonally across her body, at ease. She waited for what he would say on the subject.

He shrugged. "It's a mystery. How some people find it and others don't. You work hard at it. You work to stay together. But there's something there, too—not just familiarity—something I guess you can't create if there isn't some spark or some seed there in the first place." He was thinking of the early letters from Evelyn. She had written, "Clear across the ocean I feel the tug of the line that connects us." Hadn't he, too—no matter what he went through—felt that strong line out to her, even before they were married?

He looked at his daughter. "It's more than a feeling," he said. "People have to work at it."

"I shouldn't have married him," Marlie said. "I did it for you and Mama. I wanted to make you happy." She swung the maul and chopped. "And me, too. I thought I could be happy." She chopped. "I thought I could make it work." She chopped. "If I tried hard enough." She chopped. "Stayed busy enough." She chopped.

A funny way to talk about marriage, Russell thought. Most people tried to carve out quiet hours to be together.

He asked, "Was he going out on you?"

"No, Daddy."

He wanted to ask if she was going out on him but couldn't bring himself to it. He didn't want her to have to lie. He hoped she had been faithful, but these days you could never tell. She had waited a long time to marry—and they figured she had chosen the one she wanted. They felt relief. They could pack whatever other fears they'd had in a trunk. She had finally found someone who suited her and maybe grandkids would be on the way.

"Did you all see a counselor?" Nowadays that's what people did.

"We tried that," she said.

What Russell heard were notes of the past tense. He firmed his lips and sighed and waited for whatever else might follow. He waited the way you wait to hear from a president who's taking you to war. He wanted reasons. He wanted convincing. But because it was his daughter—and not a military leader—he figured his heart would kick in and tilt him to side with her.

And didn't he want her to have love, too? Not just security but love. He wanted that for both his children—Frank hadn't found it yet either. But it was not always easy, love. He thought of the times when he and Evelyn had quarreled. Or when he had stayed late at work—with a restlessness. He had wanted to be alone, but she worried he was with someone else. Yet for all that, most of the years were years when they'd collapsed into each other's arms, with the outside world, their parents, their children, all the burdens too heavy for them to bear alone easier to carry together.

Marlie was rolling one of the logs toward the chopping block with her foot. "There'll be some changes, you know," she said.

"I would expect." He was glad he'd taught her to change flat tires and fix leaky faucets. Out in the country, that was how you raised daughters. There was no telling which husbands might take a wild hair and abandon them, maybe with kids to boot.

"What if I told you I caught him wearing my clothes?" Marlie said, just before she swung the maul.

It took him a minute to understand what she'd said.

After her swing, she repeated it. "What if I said he was wearing my clothes? That he's decided he's a woman trapped in a man's body? That he's going to have a sex change."

"Alan?"

She swung again. "I know it must sound ridiculous to you."

He let out a low whistle. It was the kind of thing you saw on Oprah.

"People don't really do that, do they?" he found himself saying. But what he meant was, people *we know*. Sure, people in other places got caught up in snares like that. But not anyone in his realm of acquaintances. Alan, while he wasn't what you'd call a cowboy, wasn't really a sissy either.

"He's been good to me," Marlie said. "I love him. But not in a marriageable way."

Russell thought of what Alan had put her through, five years in a sham marriage. Wasting her time. No wonder there were no children. He felt a flash of anger that he tamped, tamped, tamped down to frustration. Then he went to thinking about Alan, whom he'd taken a sincere liking to. How could a young man let himself get derailed like that? Who put such ideas in their heads? Evelyn, he knew, would say it was the devil. Probably it came from TV, the sitcoms and movies, all the crazies in Hollywood. Things were all the time getting worse, you couldn't deny it. Still, he could remember way on back, in his youth, he'd seen Bob Hope and Milton Berle, from time to time, wearing dresses. But wasn't that all for the sake of a joke?

"Where did he get a notion like that?" Russell asked.

"He—just—figured it out," Marlie said, clomping. Pausing. Clomping.

"Been better if he'd figured it out sooner," Russell said. "Would have
saved you some trouble."

"Maybe he suspected it, but fought it," she said. "Maybe he was in de-
nial."

"Probably been best to keep on denying it," Russell said.

"It's no crime, Daddy." She said this in a pleading sort of way, and he
couldn't understand why she was bent on defending someone who'd so
clearly wronged her. He imagined her life with him. Him wearing her
clothes. Them pulling from the same underwear drawer. That was too
much.

"He's been awfully unhappy," she said. "He's gone a lifetime wishing
he was in a different body."

It was a crime against nature, Russell thought, but he didn't say it.
Surely, Marlie would come to see it as she gained distance. You didn't
raise your children to do those kinds of things—or *feel* that way. How
could you begin to conceive of yourself as separate from your body?
What explained that? You put your children in Sunday school, brought
them up in church, taught them the Bible, but when they got out loose,
tossed to and fro, they lost sight of the way things were meant to be.
When they were little, it was stray kittens and pups they brought home.
But when they got older, it was stray ideas that were hardest to get shed
of, like poisonous snakes in their pockets.

"Do Bob and Mavis know?"

"Not yet," Marlie said.

"It will break their hearts," Russell said.

"I guess that's why he hasn't told them," Marlie said.

"He ought to rethink it more. It might even kill them." Russell tried
to imagine their reaction. At first, they wouldn't—couldn't—believe
it. How could you? But later, as the seriousness dawned on them, they
might think it was worse than death. And it *was* a death, really, when you
considered. The loss of your son. And maybe—and this was the kind of
spin Oprah would put on it—maybe you could think of it as a birth, too.
A new daughter. But just a regular person couldn't be expected to come
around to that himself.

"Can't you see how strong he must feel about it," Marlie said, chopping, "to be willing to risk so much? He feels dead—that's what he says—and just wants the chance to live, as he feels inside." She wiped her brow and kicked the split logs out of her way.

Russell was sweating, too. He pulled off his jacket and lay it on the log beside him. He said what he was thinking: "But God wouldn't make a mistake and put you in the wrong body. How could that happen?"

Marlie's face was red from the work. "He doesn't see it as a mistake. But as a trial—and—a mission. Something he's been given to go through, something he can help others with." She put her foot on the log in front of her and gently rocked it back and forth. Then she looked up, and just for a moment, met his eye. "Besides, isn't it supposed to be the soul God's interested in? Isn't it the inside that counts?"

It was too much to absorb. Evelyn wouldn't buy it, Russell knew, convinced as she was that God didn't create homosexuals either. Though in that regard, at least, you had to admit there were examples of them in nature. It was true, too, in his lifetime, he'd owned a few she-dogs who always lifted their hind legs and peed like boys—that was the way Josie did. He was sure Marlie would explain it to Evelyn as she was explaining it to him, and he would try to help if he could, as much for Evelyn's sake as for Marlie's. Evelyn and Marlie had their confidences, he knew, just as he and Frank did. He wasn't called on much as a middleman between them. He thought of Evelyn back in the house now with the photos spread out on the bed. Probably they would do away with the ones of Alan. It would be something they'd want to forget. But Alan's parents wouldn't have that option.

"When's he going to tell them?"

Marlie shrugged, then took a half-hearted swing at the log before her. The maul wobbled when it struck the wood, and barely went in. By that, Russell knew Marlie's arms were turning to rubber. It would make the job more dangerous.

"He's afraid," she said. "Afraid they won't love him anymore."

"It'd be hard," Russell agreed and tried to imagine it.

Marlie lifted the maul, then lowered it again to rest. "You mean it'd be hard to tell them? Or it'd be hard for them to love him?"

Russell thought a minute. "Both, I guess."

Marlie raised the maul and took aim. Clomp. Clomp. Pause. Clomp.

Clomp. Pause. Though the log was one of the largest, Marlie didn't use the wedges this time but halved and quartered—and even split it into eighths—through sheer doggedness. He had figured her wrong with her tired arms. But surely, if not her arms, then her back must be strained to breaking. It made his back hurt, thinking of it.

At his feet, Josie sighed and stretched and rolled. Russell rubbed her shaved belly with the sole of his boot. Her scar was pink and healthy. He thought of Alan. The young man's body would probably be mutilated. It wasn't the same thing, of course. You did it to your pets to control the population and maybe to save them some agony in the long run. But by limiting them, maybe you took from them pleasure, too, what they might have had if left alone to nature. One way or another, people found ways to play God.

Marlie cleared the ground around the chopping block, piling the split logs in the back of the trailer. There was only one log left from the gnarled hickory; it was the base of the trunk. Surely she'd have to use the wedges for it.

"Why don't you rest a spell?" he said. "You can tackle the last one in a few minutes."

"I'm gonna try and finish," she said. "If I stop, I might not be able to start again." She took a deep breath, then bent over and commenced rolling the log with her hands. When she got to the chopping block, she stood up, looked Russell's direction, then rubbed her chin with her hand. She smiled weakly. "Daddy, it's not true," she said. "Alan's not wearing my clothes. He's not having a sex change. But it *is* true we're getting a divorce."

Russell grappled to sort out the truth from the lie. It was like isolating and capping the hot wire when you changed a light fixture—having about it all the urgency and trepidation that went along with that.

"Is he *gay* at least?" Russell asked. He'd never said the word before.

"No," Marlie said. "He's about as straight as they come."

"But why—?" He didn't even know the words to ask about the ordeal she'd just put him through. Was it to make the truth of the divorce easier to bear? He felt some relief and started to smile, but he knew he couldn't rid the puzzlement from his face. He felt cheated, like Marlie had stretched him unnecessarily. And him with a bad heart, on top of it. It wasn't like her. For whatever she was, she had always been a kind person, a compassionate person, the most sympathetic he knew.

"I just wanted to see what you'd say," she said. "See if you'd understand—and if you could find a way to love him through something like that."

She bent down and half-wrestled, half-heaved the last log up toward the chopping block. She took some of its weight, and just as he was about to protest, he caught sight, the corner of his eye, some glint, some light that might have hit the edge of the maul and ricocheted toward him. There was something in her gesture, something about the way her arms, in a familiar motion, took and handled the weight of the log, that struck him as a move his son, Frank, would make, and suddenly he recognized what she'd been getting at. He'd been making his way through a dense pine grove and had stepped, unexpectedly, into a clearing where the light was so bright and the air so sharp that it burned his eyes and stung his lungs and splintered his heart where the stitching had been. The burn and the sting and the splintering radiated outwards from his core and filled him with heat and nausea.

He started to ascend and hover. Old navy buddies had reported it, when they'd seen sudden action. How you would rise above yourself to adjust to the horror around you. He felt paralyzed. He could no more have reached down to pick up Josie's stick than he could have tossed it a couple of feet in front of her. He wanted to believe Marlie was joking. In a few years it would be funny to tell at the dinner table. Then it dawned on him he might not be there to laugh about it. And probably she would have forgotten, would have moved on to something else. He started to smile. But the look on her face—while she wielded the maul high in the air above her head—said she wasn't joking. The seriousness crept in. How could he stop her? Why need she cause them such grief? He felt a sagging weight in his shoulders. She was his daughter. He didn't need, or want, another son. Surely she had swung too far one way and would swing back again. He could see ahead rooms of heartbreak and confusion. The neighbors would view them with pity. His heart would not be able to bear it—Evelyn's heart would not be able to bear it. This would be the thing, the very thing, that put them in their graves.

The maul trembled in the air above Marlie's head. How long could she hold it vertical? He saw the strain in the way her arms shook, the pale terror that flashed across her face. For a moment, he was afraid she would drop it straight down, ripping her skull in two, ending it there, with the sawdust and woodchips hungry to soak up blood. Then he envisioned the split—that what it came down to was saving himself and Evelyn or saving her. She shifted her eyes from the log to him. She waited for an answer. The maul stayed suspended above her head.

"I wouldn't understand," Russell said. "I couldn't." How could anyone? His eyes stayed fixed on Marlie's face, and he felt a surge of heat run through his chest, stirring him. "But I would try to love," he said. "I would try to—love."

FEEDING INSTRUCTIONS

You'll have to adjust, maybe even make some sacrifices—depending on the life you've lived before—but soon you'll slip into a pattern the way a cow or goat, on her way home for milking, furrows a hillside by taking the same route again and again. I've been nine years trying to find a formula, going by instinct mainly, just doing what needs to be done. You may find yourself better suited for it than I am. But don't worry if that's not so in the beginning.

You won't have trouble with her. She sleeps eighteen, maybe twenty, hours a day, and even awake, she lies motionless in bed—curled up the way of beans left long on the vine. Through the rails sometimes, she'll watch—say if you're folding towels and sheets in the living room beside her. But she can't see well. Look at her eyes. I always thought them the color of orange pekoe tea—after you dunk the teabag a few times. Now the color is fading behind clouds of cataract. Probably she will make out your shape. She knows me—inasmuch as she knows anyone—in a dim way, by my movements and voice.

You might talk to her, tell her about the weather. We have three dogs— Scamp, Fritz, and Lady—but she may know earlier ones better: Speck, Tanner, Duke, Rover, Buddy, and Foxie. Tell her funny things they've done. Make up things if you need to. Tell her they caught a rabbit or treed a coon. Repeat, over and over, to her, "Them's good pups." That's what Martin's daddy always said, and it will be familiar. We don't have a cat, but occasionally she sees one and enjoys stories about it—call it Kasey, Sam, or Tiger-Boots. You might get her to grin—if she thinks you're tickled. To be honest, it's one of the few rewards. She may not know what you're saying, but a humorous tone stirs amusement in her.

She won't raise up. Look at her. She hasn't moved since you got here. She stays balled up like this most of the time. We keep the pillow between her knees so she won't get a bedsore. And you can see how thin her skin is—like the flesh of an overripe peach. A hand around her wrist will bruise her, and any kind of friction will peel back skin. Gentleness is a must.

Come back this way to the kitchen, and I'll show you where everything is. Her ears are still sharp. Maybe she doesn't grasp what we say, but I do my best not to alarm her. One day last week one of her sisters stood over her, saying, "Poor, pitiful thing. Wonder why she don't just go on, June?" Though I judged Mommaw—that's what our children call her— to be asleep, I asked Myrtle if she'd heard the dogs in the night, and while she was answering, I ushered us to the front porch. People don't realize, I guess, that some part of her may understand. She never wanted to burden anybody, and even now we don't want her to feel unwanted. Who knows why she hangs on?

If you watch her long enough, you'll see she can't lift her hand to scratch her nose, much less feed herself. She won't turn over—she can't. She won't try to scoot down to the foot of the bed and get out, like I've heard some will do. She's just not able. You'll have to turn her every two hours or so. Just pull up on the sheet and roll her. She's not heavy. I believe she'd stay in one place till kingdom come if we let her. She doesn't have strength to move anymore. We never used restraints, though no doubt in the beginning these might have helped. What we've done is just let her run out of steam. She had more steam—and still does—than any of us thought. It wouldn't surprise me if she outlived us all, but you can tell she's going down.

Gone are the days when she would appear on our back porch, rap on the door, and yell through the rusty screen that a strange man was eating stewed cabbage at her table. Well do I remember her quavering voice, the ribbon of fear she tried to modulate. Gone, too, are the days, after Martin's daddy died, when she was forever setting out on the road, a basket of cornbread in her arms, heading toward some home only she could see. A scarf tied around her head, she resembled those villagers you watch on

TV, the ones filing into exile from some unstable country. In those days, she was driven, let me tell you. I don't mean we drove her—oh, sometimes we did. Sometimes we had to. She would hound us till we gave in and tucked her in the car, steered up the road, and showed her all the houses, two belonging to sisters. One of them died last year—but that's nothing we will tell her now.

"Show us where you live," I'd say.

"Why, I'd talk about it. You know where I live, June. Why won't you take me home?"

"We just left your home."

"You fellas is crazy. After all I done for you, you play tricks on me. You just want the house. But I'll tell you something—." She shook her finger. "You're not gonna get it. You won't get it if it's the last thing I see to."

"Do you want to visit Myrtle or Zelma?"

"Is Zelmie home?"

"She's at *her* house. Right here." The thick planks clacked and rattled as we rolled over the bridge.

"No, no. I want to go home, June. Quit this nonsense and take me home."

Sometimes we'd coax her out to visit, hoping something would click. In no time, though, we were in the car, strapping a seatbelt around her with Zelma waving from the porch and her little cat, Ralph, going round her legs. Both were widows and might have kept each other company, but neither would have been satisfied living in the other's home.

On the way back down the road, she'd spy her house—this house. I don't think it was the white cinderblock—or our red brick beside it—as much as it was the location, the house stretched out longways, sloping itself gradually upward along the toe of a hill that began to rise sharply behind it. This wasn't the old house she visualized, yet it was the same hill, the same foot, where she'd been born and grown up.

"There, there. Let me off there. I hope Mommy and Poppy didn't leave for church yet. Did you tell them to wait?"

She was always wanting Mommy and Poppy. They'd been dead, fifty and sixty years, respectively. I memorized the dates. I'd have to tell her: "They're dead. It's written in your Bible. George Turner died January 16, 1935."

"Did Poppy die?" Her eyes would tear up and her nose blush red. "I can't seem to get it straight." Always this pained me, her blurred knowledge.

"He's dead," I'd say it more gently. "You won't see him no more on this side."

"No. But I miss him. Let me out at the house so I can talk to him."

"He's dead."

"Well, I *know* that!" she'd say. Easily today I hear her words and see her, angry, shaking her head: "Well"—shaking her head—"I"—shaking her head—"*know*"—shaking her head—"that!" A huff of air punctuated the sentence. Then, more softly, "But I want to see him. Let me off here at the house."

Martin would pull up the driveway, and we'd let her out. She'd walk across the worn path, in a hurry, like someone a long time hungry, just in from the fields. There was no relief in this for us—because we knew there'd be no relief for her. It would start up again, give her five or ten minutes to get inside, sit in her rocker, and then the longing would creak back in.

What was happening? Can you tell me? It was a failing of sight—but not eyesight—not then. There was a veil—the world, as if, through gauze. And with every day, every passing month—oh, there is a discernible pattern now—another layer of gauze and another and another, each layer tighter and more constricting than the last, less and less seen, less and less recognizable, less and less that was *her*.

Maybe, after Martin's daddy died, when she took a turn for the worse—snapping off like a light going out—we should have taken her to a doctor, a specialist, I mean. She told Dr. Weber she was fine. Said we were trying to take her money, money hidden in the hollow of an apple tree. Shouldn't that have told him something? She was getting forgetful, he said, tucking his clipboard under his arm. And old people simply get paranoid. He made no referrals. But today we hear about doctors who specialize in such things. Maybe we should have tried to find one. Now I can see this, for her abyss grows, day by day, separate from ours, but for the time—in the beginning—we were taken down with her, swirled around and under, skirting some kind of whirlpool, all of us struggling to stay afloat, and I could not see—there was no riverbank, no tugboat, not even a trotline strung in sight. Just daily rations—not enough to count on, not enough ever for any one of us, not for her, for me, for Martin, for our children. We were just dragged along in a merciless current.

Only now have I begun to think about it. There are breaks—lapses—the current eases. An hour might go by when I'm not changing her, washing her, laundering her bedsheets and gowns, fixing her dinner, or feeding her. Imagine a river slowing, a river with occasional hiccups—time becoming again, though not with speed, your own.

In the beginning, the labor was not so much physical as mental. You will not face this. You just need to feed her, change her, keep her clean. For us, then, there was the matter of matching wits, and, I'll be honest, she whittled us down. We never had time to grieve for Martin's daddy. Maybe that's a good thing. She kept us hopping. You wonder why I tremble? I guess you might say it's grated on my nerves. Most evenings—and it was worse in the evenings—I had to plant myself on the driveway and go head-to-head with her like a sheepdog trying to steer her around.

"When will Martin be home?"

"Not till five, Mommaw."

"I want him to take me home."

"You just left your home."

"I know that, but I want to go *home*," she said. "If I set in to walking, will you watch me? Make sure I get there?" Her pleading softened me.

"You don't need to get on the road this time of day. There's too much traffic. We don't want you getting run over or picked up by a crank." I spoke her language.

Her brow wrinkled, and frustration clouded her face the way a gray film of rain slides over the mountains and into the hollows.

"I don't know why nobody will help me," she said. "After all I've done for you fellers. All the nights I spend taking care of Grandma and the baby. Why can't somebody do me just one favor?"

More than anything this triggered something in me. I didn't know then all I would do, all she'd require of me. I only knew how much I'd already done. "Who do you think we're taking care of?" I'd ask. "Are you blind? Can't you see everything we do is for you? Looks like you're the one ought to be grateful."

I don't know why I said it. We all have our limits. But it was nothing she could absorb. In her mind, she was perfectly healthy. There was no sense in quarreling. I had to strategize, buy time. I was in the middle of fixing supper. The children were at basketball practice or 4-H. We wanted them to have fun, to have full lives still. I was there alone. I needed Martin to get home to help.

I'd say something like, "Well, if you're taking a trip, you'd better go next door and lock the doors." I could count on her being responsible—that was always in my favor. She *wanted* to do the right thing.

She'd shuffle in her house shoes back down the trail of tamped earth to her house, while I hid her basket of cornbread up at my house. When she'd come back looking for it, I'd say I hadn't seen it. Yes, it was cruel. But I ask you, what were my options? Of course, I returned it first chance—maybe I sent her back again to check on the "baby" and then followed behind. While she was in the bedroom, I'd put the cornbread on a plate here in the kitchen. All afternoon, she'd been at it—baking a pone of cornbread to take *home*, not wanting to go empty-handed, adamant about doing her share.

Beside the cornbread, I'd set out a glass of milk, water beading on it in the humidity. I'd lay out the dish of whatever we were having besides—chicken and dumplings or pinto beans or some kind of roast. Always there were potatoes—mashed, boiled, fried, baked. That was—and is—the staple. Remember that. Even today when you fix her plate, you'll need potatoes. These days I rely on the instant kind—it's just easier:

1 pkg. of Idaho instant potatoes
½ cup of water
½ cup of milk
margarine/butter optional (I always add lots of butter)

You'll find she eats good—it will amaze you. She's got a hearty appetite—and doesn't mind being fed. Back then, in the beginning, she couldn't, or wouldn't, pass up a meal either. Every day she said the same phrases, "I'm not hungry but I might set in and eat a big bait." Seeing the plate heaped—and thinking she had done the heaping—she'd say, "Looks like my eyes was bigger than my belly."

I did all that cooking six, maybe seven years, while she could still string together sentences. Or could she? They were more like recordings, played back over and over. Always she said, "It's good to eat someone else's cooking"—like she had a different chef every day. She was polite. "Thank you, June," she'd say. "You're better paid," which was short for, "You're better paid in heaven than here on earth."

I'd fill her plate, sit her here at the table—you had to *put* her here. I'd scoot the chair close so she couldn't stand without effort. Then I'd slip out the door, edge my way up against the house, peek in the window. Sometimes she would stick the whole plate in the refrigerator—or the oven— and I'd have to come back in, start all over. But once she commenced, she rarely left halfway through—I'd have time to run back and feed Martin and the children, who were home by then. We tried having her eat with us, or us with her, but that didn't satisfy her either. Most evenings, I ate apart from everyone—standing at our kitchen window, watching her house. When I started the dishes, I'd be looking out the window, waiting for her to come out, searching again for home. When she appeared, I'd send one of the children out to distract her.

Sometimes we just let her go. There was nothing else to do. We'd corralled her five, maybe ten times, and we just couldn't keep doing it. Not without losing our minds. We'd watch her go. We'd hold our breaths. When she was in motion, it was hard to stop her. Folks got used to seeing her. Everyone knew, sooner or later, what we were going through. I don't know what they said, passing her—the road is so narrow in the curve there. Maybe it was along the lines of, "It's a shame they can't keep her off the road," or, "Too bad it's come to this for them."

We're a small community; you can probably tell. People are good-hearted. Lots of us take care of parents and grandparents, aunts and uncles. It's the way we were raised. Sometimes a neighbor would pick her up, bring her back. But most of the time, no one could stop her. She was just bent on going. Her body took on this mechanical determination— it was uncanny. Robotic. Like she was in a daze, brainwashed. She was eighty-five then. Have I already told you this?

That she was leaving home, what'd been her home for forty years, was something she could not fathom. But there was a home somewhere. In her heart she knew it. Does she see it now? It's a good question. But you can't really ask. Or expect an answer from her. The other day she said, "This is a pretty house," like she'd never seen it before. It *is* a pretty house. She and Martin's daddy built it, both of them carrying cinderblocks. She used to tell me about the work—before she got like this. I love the wide, beveled trim around the windows and doors, this reddish-brown stain. And the hardwood floor. Martin remembers helping his daddy lay the floor—he would have been in high school then. Of course, you can see it needs to be refinished. The years with the walker and the wheelchair and the bed, the potty chair, and now the lift, all these have chafed off the color. Not to mention the puddles she made. I'd get her to the bathroom, wash her and change her clothes, while Martin went around with the blue-handled mop and a bucket of Murphy's Oil Soap. That was in the evenings. During the daytime I did it all myself. But I don't know why I'm telling you this. You won't have to worry about it. The hard part is done.

She will sleep in there under the tent I've fashioned with a sheet across the bed rails. Even in the summers I keep her covered—but cool. She can't tell you if she's hot or cold. You just have to sense it—like with a child. Sometimes she rubs her fingers together—I think she's stringing beans. Sometimes she gently swirls her hand around like she's stirring some pot on the stove. When Martin's daddy died, we could see him planting beans, pinching one or two between his forefinger and thumb, dropping each into the soil, reaching to pick up the next one. When you see something so familiar, so ingrained in them, surfacing like that at the end, it breaks your heart.

This isn't the place to start, and I apologize. You need to know what to feed her. Really, it's not so complicated. You boil chicken—any meat will do. She's anemic, so it's essential to put red meat on her plate sometimes—though you'll still have to give her iron, in liquid form, either an hour before meals, or two hours after:

2 tablespoons of iron
¾ cup of cranberry juice

The iron stains everything. Wipe the rim and bottom of the bottle—or you'll get a red ring on the counter. It's not a good idea to substitute orange juice for cranberry—the acid is too hard on her. You wouldn't want prune juice either. You don't want to upset an equilibrium it's taken months, years even, to establish. Cranberry juice doesn't affect her either way, and you need balance. That's what the Imodium's for. You go a few days handling about all you can handle—and her, too, handling what she can handle—everything goes right through her, comes out liquid like a newborn's mess. Maybe it's because everything's pureed to start with, I don't know. But there's a limit. Too many times a day, too many days in a row, and her bottom starts turning red, and there's the risk of bedsores.

Janice, the aide from the medical group, said it was all right to control her bowels, stop the flow for a day or so, with Imodium. Just remember, you're the one in charge—you and God, I guess. Mix the Imodium—not too much and not too often—with pudding:

1 teaspoon of Imodium
2 tablespoons of pudding, vanilla or butterscotch

Martin is the one told me you might be interested. Says you've always had a good heart, that you like helping people in a bind. All along I've said we could do it ourselves—we don't really have the money to pay anybody—and in a few months after the surgery, I'll be able to relieve you. I don't think it'll take as long to recover as they say. It's true I could use a vacation—but what kind of vacation is it when you're laid up? Martin says I'll get some much-needed rest, and he's probably right. It will feel good to sleep later in the mornings, knowing she's in able hands. Knowing I don't have to wake up to clean her, that I can stay in my own house.

But you shouldn't be afraid to ask for help. All the buttons on the phone ring in at our house. Martin wired it that way when she was calling everyone—calling strangers even—to take her home. I'll be able to tell you where things are—though most everything you need is here in the kitchen. Don't be afraid to call. You have to take care of yourself. I've known plenty of people who've gotten down trying to do for someone else. Your health's important, too.

You will worry. There'll be plenty of nights you'll lie awake fretting about her bowels or about a bedsore on her hip or shoulder or knee. Don't be alarmed at her body. Maybe you will be at first. She reminds me of the photos of people in starving countries. You can make out her skeleton, the knobby elbows, the knobby knees, the shape of her skull, the eyes set deep in. We feed and feed her—but I guess this is just the way of it. You mustn't think she's losing weight on your account. All you can do is feed her—and maybe pray that God takes her. I don't know if I'm supposed to say that. Don't know if I'm supposed to *think* it even. Probably it's selfish talk—and will you forgive me for saying so? It's been a hard nine years—almost a decade of my life. But why should my last nine years have been any better than her last nine years? I guess my question is: why didn't either of us have nine years better than what we had?

Feeding her, you will want to plan ahead:

7 or 8 skinless, boneless chicken breasts
1 can Campbell's low-sodium chicken broth
Boil the chicken breasts in the broth
Tear the chicken in small pieces
Puree in a food processor
Add broth as needed

She will eat about two tablespoons of pureed chicken with her potatoes. Wrap, in little foil packages, a week's worth of pureed chicken. Freeze, in these convenient sizes, everything but what you need the first week. Do beef the same way. Don't try fish—you don't want to risk bones. Whatever meat you use, moisten it with gravy. Here in the refrigerator, I've already got a jar opened. Just warm a few dabs on the stove. Warm everything on the stove—or in it. We can't have a microwave because she's got a pacemaker.

Naturally, as I said, there are potatoes. Of her fondness for them, she used to explain, "It's the Irish-man in me," but you won't hear that now. It's something you might mention while you're feeding her—it will be familiar. Lately, I fix only instant. Can she tell the difference? They're high in sodium, and that's a mark against them. But she always salted everything, just shook the shaker around a whole plate of food: fried squash, potatoes, green beans, chicken and dumplings, creamed corn, you name it. I fix instant because there isn't time to peel real potatoes—and maybe not the energy it requires—not enough to stand around waiting for them to boil, or to mash them. I know it doesn't sound like much. Maybe it will be different for you. In case it's not, you can just read the package:

1 pkg. Idaho instant potatoes
½ cup water
½ cup milk
butter (it's optional but I always add a bit)

Now, you have meat and potatoes. I don't give her many green vegetables for reasons I've already explained. You'll see what I mean. Risk it if you want. You're the one in charge now. I'm just telling you how I've done, what's worked for me. You might try mashing green beans or green peas—but I wouldn't chance broccoli or spinach. For sure, give her a big helping of applesauce with a slice of white bread crumbled up tiny. Sprinkle sugar over it like it's a cobbler. This is for bulk. Give her as much as you like. Give her anything you like—or that you think she will eat and be able to swallow. It should not be too dry or too runny. Are her meals bland? Repetitive? She gets chicken and beef a lot. For us, there is variety: McDonald's or Arby's or Long John Silver's or Taco Bell, food Martin picks up on his way from work. Sometimes on Sundays I try to fix a big meal—but lately it's been too much trouble. Like her, I guess I'm relishing someone else's cooking.

Everything must be fine—pureed and somewhat liquid. Here on the counter is the food processor. Be careful washing it because the blades are sharp. It's been years since her teeth fit. Be glad you don't have to worry with them. She used to dunk them in a cup of water and hide them in the kitchen cabinets or once up here in the freezer. They might have froze and broke if we hadn't found them.

Even with her teeth, we had routines. Are you tired of hearing about it? Probably there are things you need to do. Maybe you'd like to unpack? We hate to ask you. I wish we didn't have to. But we don't have anybody else. The children help in the summers when they're home from college. But my doctor says this surgery shouldn't wait till summer, and we don't want them to have to leave mid-semester. If you can help for just a couple of weeks, till I've recovered, I'm sure we'll get back on even footing.

But let me explain about her teeth. I don't get to talk about it much. At church they ask, "How's Grace?" And I always say, "She's just the same." Is there time to tell them all about it? And where would I start?

Do you know how many visitors she gets? Four regular ones—every Christmas. There's a man who comes and plays the banjo. Then there's one dresses as Santa Claus. The others drop off their fruit baskets at the door. The rest of the year, there's a man and his wife from church who visit, at least every other week. Mayward and Glennis are their names. They've always been ones to see to the shut-ins. There will be a crown for them in heaven. Religion pure and undefiled, you know, visiting the widows and orphans.

I guess people think we don't want company. Maybe we don't. We've got this schedule. If someone interrupts it, everything's thrown off. There are certain hours when she eats, when she takes her iron. It's what she's used to. It's what we're used to. Probably it doesn't seem like a big deal, whether there's a schedule, whether there's company. It's been nine years. If I say that when something like this happens, you get abandoned, will you believe me? People stop calling. It's just as well—you are tied to the house. You can't go anywhere—and leave her lying? People go on with their weddings and baby showers. It's easy to forget about the dying when the dying take so many years dying.

I know I need to go over her diet with you. See, I used to give her eggs and bacon and toast. It's what she grew up eating, what she loved. And oats. She loved oatmeal. We'd get her out of bed, Martin and me, take her to the toilet. I'd stay and coax her to use the bathroom—she couldn't even remember what to do. I'd say things like, "Go ahead and use the bathroom, Mommaw," and "Don't you have to pee? Go on, then," and, "Let the water fly"—things she used to tell the children. "Make your kidneys work," and, "Go on, empty your bladder. Didn't you say you needed to use the privy? Well, here you are." I'd repeat these phrases in different sequences. My daughter said it was like trying to find the key—a code that would unlock her mind. She wouldn't keep the Depends on at night, so the bed was wet, too—that was before the hospital bed. Do you know how many times I changed the bed back in her bedroom? There were three or four solid years of that—times 365 days—when she couldn't get up but could still manage to take off her Depends. I mean, sure, you do that for a child, but with children, you know they'll grow out of it.

Anyway, in the bathroom, I'd wash her face, comb her hair, present her teeth—what we'd had to coax from her the night before. Please understand, Martin's mother, in her right mind, would never have thought of going a day without cleaning her teeth. It was unthinkable. She was one of those ladies kept Listerine in business. But you see what happens. I don't know why. It just does. I had the awfullest time getting her to put her teeth in.

"Them's not mine, June," she'd say.

"Of course, they're yours. Who else's would they be?"

Sometimes she'd whisper to me, "Them's not hers." For a while, that threw me. Then I figured she was talking about the woman in the mirror.

As long as I understood where she was coming from, I could work with her.

"They are hers," I'd say. "She wants to put her teeth in, doesn't she?"

"She says she doesn't know," she'd whisper. Eventually, if I begged long enough, she'd dip her fingers in the cup, bring out the top plate, put it under the running water. She'd rub her fingers all over, cleaning the gums, the fronts and backs of all the teeth. She'd do it, over and over and over, while I stood by, holding the cup with the bottom plate.

"Put them in your mouth, Mommaw. Put them in your mouth."

Sometimes she'd slip the dentures back in the cup, and we'd have to start all over. Sometimes she'd stick the top plate in the bottom of her mouth. So many days I couldn't make her understand. Pitiful thing. I don't know why anybody has to go through it. God has his reasons, I guess. It was nothing she deserved. I used to say maybe it was sent my way so I'd learn to be more patient. But I don't think that anymore. I'm no more patient than before. If anything, I'm less so. I get aggravated easy. I cry. I fuss at her: "Why won't you pay attention? Swallow your food. Swallow. Swallow. Swallow. Swallow."

How hard can it be to swallow?

For breakfast you can give her Cream O' Wheat with tiny, tiny, tiny, pieces of buttered toast crumbled in:

1 pkg. of Instant Cream O' Wheat
1 cup of boiling water
one piece of toast, buttered and crumbled

When you feed her, put a bib on her—we use a dishcloth—with a paper towel. The paper towel takes care of little spills and keeps the dishcloth clean. But the dishcloth is for anything major. Call it a napkin. Don't say "bib" in front of her.

Before you give her breakfast, you must clean her from the night before. Would you eat your breakfast in dirty drawers? Even on the days Janice is coming to bathe her, you still need to clean her. Sometimes it takes a strong stomach. I never thought I had a strong stomach—but you do what you have to. Tell her you're changing her clothes. There's no use telling her she wet herself or that she soiled herself. Why remind her? If she doesn't remember—if she doesn't know—why bring it up, only to cause her momentary shame? She would not wet the bed if she could help it. She wouldn't soil herself. None of it is willful.

For a while, when she could walk, I would march her, walker and all, into the shower stall. Always there were the same arguments: "Don't get my hair wet. I wasn't dirty. I just took a bath last night. It's cold. Turn up the heat. Shut the door. Don't let him—unspecified—in. Wash my back. Did you wash my back? While you're at it, June, wash my back. Hurry up. She don't see no sense in this. She wasn't dirty. She just took a bath this morning." Sometimes she said "she" when there was no mirror.

And my words: "You've got to wash your hair. We haven't washed it for a week. It's dirty, Mommaw. Tell me about when you and Zelma were growing up. Did you help hang the tobacco? Who climbed to the highest logs? Here's a washcloth. Tell her to wash good. She doesn't want to stink now, does she? I'm not looking. What would I see that I haven't seen before?"

But I was telling you about breakfast. After she's clean and you put a fresh housedress on her—these are slit up the back like hospital gowns— use the lift to move her to the chair. The lift is a lifesaver, you will see. We used to grasp her, Martin and me, under the arms, raise her to sitting, then raise her to standing. We dragged her upright—you cannot say "walked"—to her chair. I still haven't recovered from all that lifting. But you'll see. The lift will save you a lot of trouble.

Scoot your chair up beside her. If you want to watch TV, you can. *Good Morning, America* and *The Today Show* are my favorites. You get the news for the day, and you see familiar faces. People laughing. They start to feel like old friends. Over time, you learn about their families, their hobbies. And like I say, they laugh. They smile. It helps.

Most days she will eat well. You raise the spoon to her face. She opens her mouth. She works on swallowing while you lift another spoonful. I think she likes the warmth of Cream O' Wheat. It must be comforting. She likes to eat. It's the only activity of her day where she's a full participant. And while you're feeding her, you can tell her about the weather and the dogs and cat. You can tell this pleases her.

If you get her on a bad day, you'll have to coax her to eat. Sometimes she's groggy or preoccupied. You say: "Open your mouth. Open your mouth. Here's your food, Mommaw. Open your mouth. Good. Swallow.

Swallow. Here's some more. Swallow. Did you swallow? Swallow your food." On these days, you'll have to turn off the TV. It will take everything you have—and more. Some days you just have to walk away, try later. Pray for patience. Fussing will not help. I know this but sometimes forget. Or maybe I don't forget—I just fuss anyway: "Why won't you eat? Your food's getting cold. If you don't care, why should I? Some people would be grateful to have food. Looks like you'd be more grateful."

Sometimes, fussing, you might strike the right chord. You'll see her mouth open—it's like a shy baby bird's mouth—innocent, trying its best, trying to please you. It'll make you feel low. She opens her mouth because you're upset, and some part of her is moved by that. Can you see the effort it takes? In those moments, you know, deep in your heart, she's doing her best. But so are you. Forgive yourself and go on.

For lunch, mash a banana and crumble some bread or cake in it. She loves bananas. Used to be, you'd offer her one, and she'd say, "Not just one. Bring me a bushel." She's crazy about them. The way I figure, she's got only a handful of pleasures. Bananas are one of them. Even so, it's getting to where she has a hard time swallowing them—swallowing anything. I don't know if it's in her mind—like she's forgetting *how* to swallow—or if it's a physical problem with the esophagus.

Surely you'll see, though, it's one of her last strongholds in the world. She tries desperately to swallow. Watch the way her chin quivers. When her mouth's full, it's all she can do to hold her lips closed. Her lips tremble from the strain. And sometimes, she loses it, and food dribbles out. Or she balances it in her mouth, then works up her energy at the back of her throat, poises herself, finally swallows. It's a relief to her—and to you— every time. Praise her for it. Tell her what a good job she's done. I think, for her, it may very well be the feat of the day.

When the children were small, they'd laugh when she drank water and sometimes there was a noise in her throat—like with anybody— but she'd comment on it, say, "My swallower is a-squeegling," and the children thought it was funny. I guess *squeegling* was like a squeak and a screech and a jiggle all in one. I don't know where she got the word or if she made it up. She was always saying things to make us laugh. But giving her liquids is where you'll have the most trouble. Sometimes these go down her windpipe—and it leads to respiratory infections. Prop her

straight up—as straight as she'll go, whether it's in the hospital bed or
chair. Do not, whatever you do, tip her head back. Keep her in a position
where her chin is close to her chest. It got to the point where she was getting strangled with every sip. We had to start using Thick-It, this cellulose
powder. Janice brought us a big can. You mix it in a cup of water or cranberry juice. Use it with every liquid, even the juice that's the vehicle for
iron:

1 teaspoon Thick-It per cup = thin Cream O' Wheat consistency
2 teaspoons Thick-It per cup = thick Cream O' Wheat consistency

At bedtime, we give her orange sherbet laced with medicine—you
have to use a pill crusher for this—it's over here on the counter beside the
Thick-It. Kind of a grooved mortar and pestle. The pill grains get caked in
the grooves, and you have to scrape out the grooves with a toothpick. She
doesn't take much medicine—just a heart pill and Lanoxin. I've always
wondered if Lanoxin contributed to her forgetfulness. Years ago, I read
an article in the newspaper suggesting memory loss was a side effect. She
started taking it when she had passing-out spells in her seventies—right
before they put the pacemaker in. But why would a doctor prescribe a pill
to get oxygen to your brain if it contributes to your brain's decay? Sometimes, I wonder, too, if the pacemaker, the constant rhythm it sets, keeps
her alive maybe long after she was ready to go.

Martin has been the one to stay with her at night these last years, but
he'll be taking care of me for a week or so after the surgery—I don't think
it'll take much longer than that to recover. I feel fine. I don't see why it
can't wait till summer, to tell the truth. It's hard to imagine not being
down here, seeing to her, feeding her. But you'll be sleeping back in the
guest bedroom where you can hear her if she calls. We prop her on her
side with pillows to keep her off her back—but she thinks someone's
sleeping too close, and Martin says she'll occasionally quarrel: "Why
don't you turn over. Scoot over in the bed, Zelmie. Why do you have to
sleep so close? I don't have no room. Well, I don't know why you have to
sleep so close to a feller for."

I know some people don't have it as easy. Viney Pauley's mother tried
to get out at night—even with someone staying with her—and they had
to change the locks, so you could get in but not out. She was like a pris-

oner. But they're all prisoners when you think about it. I read now, in the papers, about a medicine to calm them, and I can think back to hundreds of evenings when a remedy like that would have been handy to us.

"Where are you going?"

"I'm going home."

"What you got in your basket?"

"I brought my things. Why don't you take me home?"

"You're going the wrong direction."

"I'd talk about it. I've lived here all my life. I've been here a lot longer than you. I know where my home is."

"Where is it?"

She'd point. It was always up the road.

"Maybe you'd better go check on the baby before you leave," I'd say.

"Is the baby still down there?"

"You said it was."

She'd turn to go. How many times? I don't know who the baby was—maybe one of our children. We never gave her a doll—though sometimes they do that in nursing homes. I guess we were trying to preserve some sense of dignity for her. But maybe it would have been soothing, having somebody to care for, a life to cherish, you never know. You look back. You don't know if you've done the right things. Maybe we should have taken her to our house—after she got bedridden. All along, though, we thought she'd be more comfortable here. I maintain there's some part of her recognizes things—maybe the wide, springing sound of the screen door opening, or the creaking of us walking across the furnace grate, the sound of the refrigerator door shutting, maybe the way the light comes in, a quality in the air.

We've done the best we could—in the moment. That's been the thing. It's always been in the moment—we've always felt cornered, like whatever we needed to do had to be done then, like there wasn't time to foresee the thing that was next approaching around the bend. There used to be video games the children played. You'd have your little figure on the screen, and different obstacles or enemies would appear, and you'd have to decide then and there what to do. It tested your reflexes. I guess that's how we've felt, like we're getting our reflexes tested.

People say they don't know how we've done it. I say, you just do what you have to. We didn't have time for a plan. We've swung by the seat of our britches since the day Martin's father took sick and then died. Yes, there were times before that, times she didn't know him, but I'm glad he didn't live to see her like this. She didn't even recognize him dying in the hospital bed there where her own bed is now. Instead, she wept for her father dying, for how he'd shrunk down to nothing. She'd been married to him fifty-four years. We had them the big golden anniversary party with a two-tiered white cake. But she couldn't see him die—or wouldn't. I guess maybe these are the same.

I don't know when we did what. At some point, Martin turned off the gas to her stove. She'd stopped making cornbread and wasn't cooking anything—we encouraged her at first—but she was leaving the flames on, and sometimes the flames would go out, and the house would fill up with gas. She couldn't smell it. At some point we took the doorknobs off the bathroom door so she couldn't lock herself in.

Then we had to hide the basement door key, afraid she'd fall down the steps. I remember one time right before that, though, when I found her down there after bringing her supper. It'd been a while since I'd been in their basement, and the mustiness, the damp earth scent, brought back so much to me. She wasn't herself, but standing there in the basement with her, I could remember her, as she had been. I could remember the two of us there, admiring our canning—the rows and rows of green beans, of stewed tomatoes, of bread-and-butter pickles, of corn, all the things we had canned together, all the food we'd gathered from Martin's father's garden. Seems like I could picture it so clearly. If you've ever canned, you know how beautiful those gleaming jars of color are—you know the greens, the reds, the yellows. And she always lined them up so straight in their separate sections. Can you imagine seeing them? Say by the light of a couple of bare forty-watt bulbs? The beans were beans we had strung together, with the cold, metal, red-rimmed white dishpans on our knees, the paring knives flashing—that scent of green pervasive. The sounds of the children's voices in the yard. The corn was corn we had shucked together. I could hear the squeaking sounds as you pulled down those tight sheaves—you know, if you've done it. And the way the fine silk hair of the corn feels, the way it clings to your fingers and hands. Martin's daddy would lay it across his upper lip for a mustache, and the children laughed—and I laughed. And occasionally, there'd be a big, fat green worm at the top of the cob—how I hated that. But I did like she did, jerking it once hard and flinging the worm to the ground, or taking one of the green sheaves, like a piece of paper, and pinching the worm off. Then, of course, we did all the chopping and cleaning, washing the jars here in her kitchen. I followed her the first few years and then, after that, knew the seasons of things.

On the day I found her in the basement, all the shelves had glass jars, but the jars were empty. A fine film of dust covered them. She was looking for something. Who knows what? The potato bins were empty. But though the potatoes were long gone, I could still smell them and remembered the early days of spring every year when we used the smallest ones, the only ones left, with their eyes sprouting.

"Are you hungry?" I asked.

"No, but I might set in and eat a big bait," she said.

"I believe supper's ready," I said. "It's on the table."

"Well, let's go and get us some." She led the way up the steep basement steps. At the top, she turned to make sure I was with her and then clicked off the light switch.

People should think of a plan. We didn't have time. Do this for a day or two, or for a couple of weeks, or months, do it for nine years and see when you have time for a plan. You do just what you need to. God helps you. Time passes quickly, as the saying is. At least, that's true when it's behind you.

And when you think about it, the future's not so far away either. It won't be long till summer—say, if I changed my mind and decided to wait and have my surgery then. Our children could help. Maybe we wouldn't have to ask you for anything. I could go on taking care of her. I think I'm going to talk to Martin about it. I feel fine really. I'm not having any trouble. None that I haven't learned to live with. I'll talk to him when he gets home from work this evening. You can wait till then, can't you? Just don't unpack anything. I'll talk to my doctor, arrange everything. I feel sure I'll be able to keep on feeding her and doing all the rest till summer comes.

As I said, nearly everything we need is here in the kitchen. There's milk and butter in the refrigerator. The pudding's in here, and in the freezer there's ice cream and sherbet. If something goes wrong, if we have to call the paramedics, there's this DNR magnet on the refrigerator. You probably noticed. They'll know what it means: Do Not Resuscitate. The nurse brought it in. We did all the paperwork about three months ago after she took a bad spell. We'd seen her sister live a year on a feeding tube—like a vegetable—and we knew we didn't want that.

I don't like the magnet, really—oh, I know it's the right thing. I just don't understand why they asked us to put it *here* of all places. Every time I open the refrigerator to get out her cranberry juice or water, I see it, and I think, is this all it's come to? All these years, all this labor, this fretting, all the nursing I've done, and now just this: Do Not Resuscitate? I don't know what it is, it just strikes me as funny. You know what I mean? But here it is on the refrigerator if we need it.

THE SORROWS YOU CAN'T ENTER

"Can you keep an eye on my dogs today?" The voice is strange, and I have to think a minute who it is. Jack and me, we're not used to speaking by phone.

"They're not acting right," he says.

"How they acting?"

"Just funny. Sluggish. One's drinking a lot of water. The other won't raise his head to look at me."

"Not the coyotes, was it?"

"Nah," Jack says. "No wounds, no blood."

"Sure, I can look in on them."

On the other end of the phone there is wide quiet.

"Jack?" I say.

"I hate to go to work," he says. "And leave them." His voice cracks. "They're real sick, Lloyd."

"No," I say. "Go on. You got that load of pipe coming. I'll get up there soon as I can."

Jack has the kind of dogs we always kept around the house. Strays that just wandered in, what people always called Heinz 57s. Loyal, usually smart, leastways about knowing a good home. When the two spotted pups come to Jack's, he was building a house in the woods on the property I sold him. He had opted for a mountain view—though it meant extra grading for the road and house seat—a whole extra year toward construction. Admittedly hard for a couple just starting out and with a baby on the way. The pups, motley as the coat of Joseph, showed up just after the wife took off with the baby.

The dogs are in a bad way. Soon as I see them I know they don't stand a chance. Ben is near gone—shuddering with spasms and taking his last breaths, deep, hard ones. His eyes are glassy and watery—looks like tears. It's not easy to watch. They are good, sweet dogs. Jack said they were sick, but somewhere deep down, he must have known they were dying. Jesse is panting hard beside Ben on the garage floor. His breath condenses on the concrete, forms a wetness on the gray.

I take Jack's extra key from the cinderblock stoop and let myself in to use the phone.

"Let me speak with Pat."

"Hold one minute, please."

On the tablet beside the phone, Jack has written the name Kathy Brumfield and a phone number. I remember this is the girl the apprentices are trying to fix him up with.

The house is clean—orderly anyway, not piled up like some houses get with only a man there. Things haven't gone well for Jack since he started building. He's a hard worker, but for some folks, that don't count for as much as it ought. I chose him—after doing my homework. With family land, you want to be careful. I had no one to inherit the property, my boy having been killed at a train crossing thirty-four years ago. I waited for the right man, one just starting out—with a good job. Someone from a respectable family and with a respectable wife. Someone not known to be a brawler or ne'er-do-well.

Jack had an earring, which I was naturally opposed to. But his hair was short, clean-cut. Won me with his conversation, deferring several times to his father, who'd recently passed away, died in his tobacco field, of a heart attack. I knew Jack's daddy—not well but knew of him. Word was, when he run out of insulation for his house in the fifties, he used burlap sacks stuffed with chicken feathers in his upstairs walls. I always wondered what some future unsuspecting occupant, maybe sawing through to put in a new light switch, would think when feathers flew out.

All in all, I don't think I made a bad choice. It wasn't long after Phyllis's funeral that I found him—but I still wish I'd had her vote on it. She had

good sense about people and maybe could have seen what was coming—
that Jack's wife would leave him for another man, saying the baby wasn't
his to start with, no matter that all along he'd been saving and scraping
together and working all those hours after his day job, well into the night,
trying to fix a house for them.

"He's back in surgery," the receptionist says. "Take a message?"

"This Sue?"

"Yes, who's this?"

"Lloyd. Lloyd Carper."

"Hey, Lloyd. What can we do for you?"

"I got a sick dog here. Want to bring him in. I think he's dying. Will Pat
be able to see him?"

"Well, he's got a lot of—"

"It's an emergency, Sue," I say. "Life and death. One dog's already
dead."

"Bring him in," she says. "We'll make time."

Jesse is dead weight. It pains me to take him from his brother, where
he's probably most at peace. But Ben's gone, not breathing now, the struggle over. And Jesse doesn't move his eyes while I carry him, doesn't care
what I do, is beyond fear—and so, I guess, past living. I haul him slowly
in the trailer of my tractor down to my barn, lay him up in my truck seat.
Jesse pants hard—the kind of race you can't run forever. His spotted belly
moves up and down.

"Just hang on, Jesse," I say. "Hang on."

The dogs come along just as Jack was nursing his wounds from his
wife leaving. Pharaoh's daughter couldn't have been happier with a babe
in the bulrushes. They give him love like only dogs could—without the
expectations humans have of one another. He named them after a team of
oxen or mules—I don't remember which—his granddaddy had owned
as a young man and reverenced later in life.

The dogs have never been mean—but curious, like to be in everybody's business. Jack hasn't been able to keep them up on the mountain. He locks them in the garage on garbage day, but that doesn't satisfy some folks. He gets calls, so-and-so, I will not say who, wanting him
to keep them penned up and off their property. Out here, though, so
many open acres to roam, you feel bad keeping a dog locked up. We've

tried hard to train them, teach them their boundaries, walking along the property line with them. Funny thing, when we're with them, they don't stray.

From the vet's office, I call Jack on his cell phone. "You got a minute?"

"Go ahead."

"I'm at Pat's, Jack. It doesn't look good."

"For both of them?"

"Doesn't look good for either one, Jack. Just prepare yourself."

"Is there any chance?"

I don't want to have to tell him on the phone. "Not much, Jack. Just be prepared."

When Jack pulls in, I'm sitting on my porch. For about a year now, he's stopped here every day on his way up the mountain, occasionally eating with me. The dogs usually wait right here to meet him, their tails fanning back and forth on the floor when they see his truck. Then while we sit, they lie on the porch, the way a dog will do, occasionally raising their eyebrows to entice you to throw them some little scrap. Today—them not here to greet him—Jack is reluctant to get out.

He's all balled up when he steps on the porch—tight-scrunched—face hard with worry. He's looking around the porch, making sure they aren't here, lying sick, some secret antidote discovered. Probably he reads my face. I've never been good at hiding things. Then everything leaves him, drops off like yellow leaves of a hickory in one of those hard October rains.

"Bennie died while I was up there," I say. "I rushed Jesse to the vet. There was nothing to be done."

He nods, sits down in the lawn chair.

"What was it?"

"Poison," I say. "It was antifreeze."

He takes a deep breath. Holds it hard. Then lets it go. He rubs his face. "Where'd they get it?"

I shrug my shoulders. "Don't know. Most people know not to leave it out."

He continues rubbing his face, as if he's trying to massage out his next words.

"I left them covered in your garage," I say. "Figured I'd help you bury them—if you want."

"Why?" he says. He leans his forehead against the porch post. "Why? Why? Why?" He bangs his head once for each why.

The Lord giveth, and the Lord taketh away. I heard it all my life. But I know enough not to say it to Jack. There's not much he will hear today.

"Come on," I say, standing. "I'll help you. There's a graveyard we've got—for pets and other animals. If you want—."

He nods.

"Let me go first," he says. "Give me about fifteen minutes."

"You sure?"

He nods again but doesn't meet my gaze.

I watch his truck struggle up the rutted mountain, hear it creak back and forth. When he's out of sight, I get on my tractor and start up the hill behind him. I want him to hear the sound of it coming. Not have time for the awful silence that comes in absence.

In my trailer are the two tarps I took off my roof when I got back from the vet's. I figured the dogs needed them worse than I do. On top of the mountain, Jack carries the dogs from his garage to the trailer—carries them like children, lays them gently on the sun-stiffened tarps. I start the engine and haul the dogs around through the woods to the cemetery. Jack walks along behind with a couple of shovels over his shoulder. The clearing is mostly in shadow now, but I park at the edge where the sun hasn't been cut off.

I shut down the engine, tell him, "The sun hits full here in the mornings. It faces east—the way cemeteries used to."

He takes a deep breath, lets it out. His eyes are full, but he's holding back.

"You want to pick the spot," I say.

"It don't matter," he says. "Wherever you say. I don't know what else is buried here."

"How 'bout over there—near the pines? They always liked to roll in the pine needles."

"Okay." He wipes his nose with the back of his hand. "I don't care really."

We both of us commence digging. Quietly. There's no need to talk.

What you hear is shoveling. The shovels scrape sandstone; they screech and grate on through. Sometimes pry up. Hit roots. Chop, chop, chop through the roots.

Jack digs hard and fast, working through it.

When he stops to get his breath, he says, "Everyone knows about antifreeze. Any dog or cat loves it. Can't resist it." He examines a sweat bee on his forearm, then flicks it off. "You don't think someone done it on purpose, do you?"

I guess you suspect the ones complained the most. But that's not a fire I want to feed. You're bound to have quarrels with neighbors. Quarrels with God, too. But Jack's young, capable of—and blind to—things that might cripple him the rest of his life.

I hold my tongue. There's a lot I won't tell him. Won't say what hard, ugly deaths they suffered. How convulsion and anguish were wrung out till the last bitter breath. How they did not understand the suffering, poor things, and could not see the end till the end was right there and took them. A burning nausea had them by the throat, set fire to their stomachs. The vet said it shut down their kidneys—all their vitals. In their eyes was prayer for it, for everything, to cease. The vet gave Jesse a shot to help him along, but by then he'd already done most of his suffering.

"This land's been in your family a long time," Jack says. "You know any stories about it?"

"Stories? I've probably told you most of them. How my great-great granddaddy settled here before the Civil War? Only a wagon and kettle and goat and horse to his name."

"Haunted stories," Jack says. "I mean, do you think this place is haunted?"

"This place? The graveyard you mean?"

"This." He stretches out his hand, pans it slowly across everything. "I mean, is it haunted or something?"

"I don't reckon it's any more haunted than any other place," I say.

"Just that since I came here—." He sticks his shovel in the ground, rests his foot on it. "Maybe I'm the one that's haunted."

I catch his meaning. "Well," I say. "I lost my wife—my son, too."

"And dogs."

"And chickens and calves and goats. Once a horse I was partial to."

"What happened with him?"

"Her. She got the colic one spring. Died. I'd bought her for my boy but seemed like all of us took to her. She'd watch you—like she could read your mind. One time she got out, stuck her head in through the loose screen of the kitchen window where Phyllis was doing dishes. We ran in to look at her. Had suds on her nose. Phyllis was laughing. Was a sight to see."

But Jack isn't listening, his mind following its own back roads. I say, "I don't know that I've lost more than any other man my age. But I can see how you might feel, Jack. Seems like it's come early to you."

"Some things is natural and some ain't. What was done to my dogs—that seems like—"

"Meanness," I say. "*Seems like* meanness and *might be* meanness. But no way to prove it."

"And nothing to do about it." He says this as a statement, simple. But behind it there's a question. He waits for some response, to see if I agree. Probably the way his daddy has taught him to listen.

Folks just protecting what is theirs, I want to say. Maybe that's one way to look at it. Might've been an accident, someone flushing out a radiator. But I don't know what to say to Jack. Sometimes you can sit back and watch it all unfold, and it will unfold beautifully. But sometimes you watch it, and it will be sheer tragedy—and then you wonder what is the one thing, the very thing, you could have said or done to prevent it?

Finally, Jack asks outright, "What should I do?"

"My boy never asked me that," I say. "He never wanted me to interfere."

"He might've," Jack says, "if'n he got pushed into a corner."

I swallow. Jack isn't keeping secrets; he's telling me where he is. I think of Rickie, the last night—how one night's words and scenes are imprinted after so many years of rerunning them. He tried to slip out the front door, gliding quietly past me in my recliner. "Why don't you stay home tonight?" I asked. It startled him. But what father wouldn't ask it of any child—no matter his age? Maybe I could have said, "Leave the beer in the bag tonight." Or, "I don't want you drinking but at least drink at the barn where you won't be on the roads." Any number of things I could have said, done. Maybe grabbed my coat, said, "Wherever you're going, I'm going with you."

I had not given up—you don't do that with your children. But I was resigned to him having to learn his own lessons. A heart bent on something is hard persuaded from it. I locked the doors at midnight, knowing his mother slipped and opened his bedroom window.

You don't know when to step in and when not to. People nowadays talk about tough love. But I tell you, if I saw a train coming down the tracks and my boy in the path of it, I'd rush out and push him off—no matter the cost to me. No one tells you the train is coming, though, till it's already gone through.

I done a little carrying on myself when I was a young man—not much—tipping outhouses, letting the air out of tires, and the like. Sampling Harry Yeager's moonshine occasionally. I don't know if times now is any worse than then—though they seem to be. Each generation's capacity for meanness seems to grow larger. And the generation before—those of us left—are kept here to witness, in amazement. My boy was unhappy. Rickie was. He kept unfolding and refolding the map, trying new routes, never finding the place he was looking for.

"No one ever done nothing like this to me before," Jack says.

"What about that fella lured away your wife?" I ask. "That was ornery, wasn't it?"

"It was," he says. "But maybe I had it coming. JoAnn's lawyer told me I was negligent. Working on the house, not spending enough time with her. Maybe I was. I don't know. I don't see how I could have done different."

Out in the woods, there is a sudden crashing, running and plowing through dead leaves. Then it stops. Both of us turn our eyes that direction. Up on the hill behind us a coyote howls.

"Someone's go'll have to kill them," I say. "They're overrunning the place."

"I hate to hear them," Jack says. "Seems like it goes right up my spine. Ben and Jesse hated them, too, always barked when one was near, raised their hackles."

"For a long time they wasn't here," I say. "DNR brought 'em in to control the deer. Of course they won't admit it. But everybody knows it."

Jack commences shoveling again. "Guess we better dig deep to keep them out."

The sun settles behind the trees, filters through the tree trunks, leaves us in pinstriped shadows. Jack keeps digging until he's dug out the dirt between the two holes and made one large grave. "They were never far apart," he says. "I reckon they'll rest better like this."

Around us rise the scents of the dark broken earth and pinesap from the roots we've busted. Jack stretches out one tarp in the bottom of the grave, then carries the dogs and places them back-to-back, against each other. No matter how many times you've seen it, the stillness in a body that's prone to motion surprises you. Bewildering, the way a living, moving being suddenly turns to object and shell, the husk that you throw away.

Jack gets down in the grave, kneels down beside them, kisses their heads. He puts a hand on each of their foreheads, like he might be checking for fever. He lifts one of Ben's front paws, rubs it like he would rub life back into it. I know the roughness he feels on the dog's padded feet. He does the same with Jesse. These are his good-byes. With a preacher, people all around, you don't feel so free. You feel boxed in, everyone keeping you in check. When I see Jack down in the hole, covering them with the other tarp like they're his babies, I can't stop the tears gathered in my eyes.

"The Lord giveth and the Lord taketh away," Jack says, stepping out of the grave. His face is all wet.

"Blessed be the name of the Lord," I choke out.

"I'm going to the house a minute," Jack says. He's about to break. "Go ahead and start covering them. Seems like I just can't."

I'm close enough that I could catch his arm, turn him to me, and hold him. But I don't. I keep my distance, respect his privacy. I've never been one to trespass on another's grief.

When he's out of sight, I start laying the earth down gentle on the dogs, saving the biggest rocks to place around on top. If there were a wife and son waiting at his house, Jack would do his best to comfort them. Losing the dogs would hurt but be bearable. He would be strong for the child, for the wife.

I wipe my eyes on my shirtsleeve, work fast so they'll be covered when he gets back. If he owned a gun, it would be harder to let him walk off. But there are other ways, I know, to dull the pain. I look up, and through the woods I see the lights come on in his house. I keep covering. I can

give him time. You have to—men do that for each other. You give lee-
way, a wide berth. But he's too young, still new to the world's blows, these
what have come all at once in a heap, to give him too much space.

Evenings after this, Jack continues stopping at my place. He's smoking
again and uses one of my Folger's cans for an ashtray. We miss the dogs
being with us, and Jack plays it back over and over.

"I guess I should have kept them penned up," he says. "But I've always
hated to see a dog in a pen. Course, I guess, it's better than a dead dog.

"If it was just the garbage, I would have picked it up every day myself
if they'd called me. Or if they'd said, this is your last chance—after this
we're going to kill your dogs. I guess I would have done different."

I say, "Maybe I shouldn't have been saving scraps for them, encouraging them to go pillaging."

"Nah," he says. "They liked coming down here. It was their second
home."

"Yeah," I say. "They was good company—even through the day after
they'd made their rounds. They'd stay here with me, help in whatever way
they could."

"Whatever they done," Jack says, "they didn't deserve this."

He stands up, goes to the corner where a moth has got itself trapped
in a spider web. If he's done it once, he's done it a dozen times. He closes
his hands around the moth, careful not to clamp its wings, then draws the
moth out in the cup of his hands. He sits back down, opens his hands on
his lap. The moth flutters free, out into the evening.

"What makes folks want to kick a man when he's down?" he asks.

"You got to quit thinking it was aimed at you—deliberately," I say.
"Even if it was, there's nothing you can do about it. You go'll have to sleep
through it. Just sleep. Even when you're awake, just sleep through your
routine, till you wake up on the other side of it."

"But I ain't sleeping," he says. "I'm awake, all hours. I'm holding Ben
and Jesse, and they're slobbering on my hand and licking the tops of RC
cans and rolling on their backs wanting their bellies rubbed and smelling
like dog. And you know," he says, "that's all I had left.

"When I finally go to sleep, the coyotes wake me up howling. I guess
Ben and Jesse kept them at bay. The coyotes come in close now. And for

all the insulation, six-inches of it, and all those double-paned windows, all that effort I made to seal up the house tight, I hear them like they was right beside my bed."

Rain or shine, the porch is where Jack and me sit. It's the most comfortable room, partway in, partway out. I cook extra and always save leftovers for him. I stash the scraps in the garbage so he don't have to see them, don't have to think of the keen pleasure Ben and Jesse would derive from them.

One evening we sit through a downpour. Around us, the Folger's cans fill up, drip by drip, some drips pretty steady.

"That's a new one, ain't it?" Jack says, pointing.

"Just a bigger one," I say. "A louder one."

"You not ready to put on a new roof yet?"

"Nah," I say. "It's not more than I can bear."

"I could help you," he says.

"It's okay," I say. "This one will last me."

"What about the next person?"

"That's for him to decide."

"Kind of shortsighted, ain't it?" he looks at me. "I don't mean no disrespect."

"I'm used to the dripping—the sound," I say. "It's like music."

Jack flicks the ash of his cigarette into the water of the nearest can.

"I see you're smoking again," I say. It's the first time I've mentioned it.

"Yeah. I was down to two a day, morning and night, when Ben and Jesse died. Now I'm back up to two packs."

Killing yourself won't help, I want to tell him, but I don't want to put the idea in his head.

"Sometimes," I say, weighing my words, "you get started in on something and can't stop. Or it's hard to. Seems like one leads to one more. The first don't satisfy, and so there's a second, and so on."

"It keeps me calm," he says. "There's a storm underneath." He pats his chest.

I think of lava, volcanoes, cracks in the earth that let things seep through.

"With the dogs, see—" he blows out. "With the dogs, they had a calm about them. Soothing. In the evenings, so glad to see me. Anxious for whatever we were going to do—in the yard or in the woods—even if we just walked. Was just a peace they had—and it would rub off on me."

The rain slackens off just as suddenly as it came, and around us, we hear the slowing drips in the Folger's cans, the drops from the leaves of the trees as they shake themselves off. The birds make last-minute calls before settling to roost. The lightning bugs start to raise up around us, one or two at first, then more. The frogs set in to singing. We sit quiet. It's near dark. There's just the glow of Jack's cigarette.

Then Jack raises his arm, points. There's a stray dog slinking just into the edge of the yard, up from the creek. It hunkers down, cautious. I can hardly see its coloring, but by its walk, I know it's not a dog I recognize. Then, as it draws closer to the house, it dawns on me: a coyote. For all the time I've been hearing them, this is the first I've seen. It looks like a dog, but is not exactly a dog.

Jack makes like he has a rifle, takes aim in the air, puts his finger on the trigger, his cigarette where the trigger would be. He hunted as a boy with his father, he's told me, but gave it up early, without the stomach or heart to follow through.

Jack keeps aim on the coyote with his invisible rifle. Then, "Ppulkhs-ksk," he makes the loud noise of a gun. The coyote raises its ears, looks to the porch, then tucks its tail, darts for the cover of the woods.

Next evening, Jack doesn't stop. And after that, doesn't stop. He smiles, waves out the open window when he goes by on his way up the mountain. I keep cooking. I cook loud things—with scents that will pass through the screen doors and saturate the yard, scents that might catch in his gut when he drives past. Fried fish. Always cornbread from Phyllis's recipe. French fries. Fried hamburgers. I cook for two. Every evening. He doesn't stop. He waves. I wave back, then watch him go, the dust whirling up behind his truck as he tackles the hill, the truck rocking in the ruts. I let him go. Maybe he's talking to Kathy Brumfield. What can I do? Can't run out and flag him down every day. He has his own life. Some sorrows you can't enter, not when the owner says off-limits. So I tell myself. There are boundaries to respect.

Eventually, though, it gets the best of me. I lose sleep myself. I lie awake. Any hour of the night I might hear the high-pitched, eerie howls of the coyotes. What if Jack has bought himself a gun? Will he remember how to use it? Remember what to do and what not to? What if he sits up there at night, waiting for a coyote to stalk across his yard, waiting, the gun coddled in his arms, the trigger warmed by his finger, waiting, waiting, thinking what use is it anyway, why even go on trying?

One evening after he's gone through, I give him time to settle, then drive my tractor back, knock on the door. He opens the door, squinting at the light.

"Jack, here's some cornbread," I say. "I made too much this evening."

"Thanks, Lloyd," he says, reaching for the warm package wrapped in aluminum foil. "But I just don't have an appetite."

He seems to have lost weight in just this short time, and there are dark circles around his eyes.

"You got to eat," I say. I try to look through the door behind him, see the shape of his house.

"I'm still sick over it, Lloyd." he says. "Just sick. I want to do something. Take action."

I wait to be invited in. But he stands in place, blocking the door, holding the cornbread. "Maybe you give yourself an ulcer," I say. "Worrying so much over it. I had one once. Seem like your whole stomach is on fire, every time you eat."

He shakes his head, then concedes, "I guess it could be."

We're quiet on the porch. Him waiting for me, me waiting for him.

"How's the new site?" I ask. "You got the underground laid yet?"

"Mostly," he says. "We're testing for leaks."

I nod. "That, uhm, Reynolds fella. He still struttin' around?"

"Nah. He got transferred. Put on a job in Huntington." Jack doesn't volunteer anything more, just doesn't open up any other paths.

"You called that Brumfield girl yet?" Soon as I say it, I know I've barged in.

"Nah. What do I got to say?"

I shrug my shoulders. "Maybe she'd do all the talking," I offer.

"Maybe," he says.

I figure Jack knows what I'm up to, and there's no sense making a fool of myself, losing his respect. "Well," I say, "stop by sometime when you get the chance." I turn away as if to leave. And when he doesn't tell me to stay put, I follow through. I walk down the steps, then swing myself up onto the tractor.

"Lloyd," he says, coming out onto the porch and leaving the door wide open. "You know, I was just sitting down there till bedtime and only coming home to sleep. I feel restless," he says. "Just need to get into something."

I nod my head.

"It's hard coming home to an empty house," he says. "You of all people know that. But I got to learn to. You got your life. Don't think you have to babysit me."

I laugh. Around here, I'm still surprised when people say what they're thinking. Generally when people speak, they leave the shadows behind their words for you to read.

"Whether you're there or not, Jack, I sit on the porch till bedtime myself. But me and the lightning bugs, seem like we don't speak the same language."

Within the week, Jack is stopping again. I have stocked up on milk—in case he has an ulcer. And I'm learning to bake instead of fry. I cut back on tomatoes.

You don't know how much you yourself can stand. And as much as you measure a man, you don't know how much he can stand either.

"I got a big house on the hill and no one to live in it," Jack says.

"You live in it."

"I got nowhere to go." He inhales. Blows out smoke. "I feel lost."

His talk scares me—but not as much as his silence did.

"What do you do when everything's been taken from you?" he asks.

I think of Job in the Bible and say, "You look for the thing that's going to come along next."

"And what if nothing does?"

"You have to wait."

"How long?"

"Sometimes a long time. Sometimes not so long."

"You sound like a politician," he says. "Or a preacher."

"I'm only saying what I know."

"I know."

One Friday evening late summer we hear a cry come out of the woods—like a child. Then it comes again and again, and the closer it gets, the more shape the sound takes until finally it resembles the bleating of a kid goat or a lamb. We hear crashing in the woods, leaves kicked up, sticks broken. Jack jumps up, runs off the porch to the back of the house, up the hill to the edge of the woods. The cry comes louder and louder.

Jack runs back down.

"You got a gun, don't you?"

"What is it?"

"Coyote after a fawn," he says.

I fetch the loaded rifle from the house, some extra shells, hand them to Jack.

"I'll go, too," I say.

His face lifts in surprise. Maybe thinks I'll slow him.

We enter the woods quiet except for breathing hard. You learn a lot about a man's character when he's carrying a gun. No matter where I walk, behind or in front, I take notice of the gun—and see that Jack always has it directed away from me. Another thing his daddy's done well teaching him.

Not far in, we step over the fawn's body. Its eyelid flutters, but there are flies already around it—like it's been hounded and running a long time. I don't expect us to find the coyote that chased it here.

Nothing but a shock, then, when we spot one so quickly. Down in a little forked hollow where three or four creeks merge and big rocks jut out in the air. Dead trees have fallen, making log bridges where the mosses can grow across the hollows. The coyote stands just out from under one of the overhanging rocks.

I feel Jack's forearm against my ribs. Stay.

He lines up the bead.

I close my eyes and want to cover my ears—but I don't move. You want for someone—that he not be killed. By cancer, by a train, by a drunk driver, or by his own hand. You pray for that. But you want, too, that he not have to kill. That he not have to step into that room—different from the one where he habitually lives, that dark cave he might be better off not entering—and from which he will have to come back stamping the blood from his boots.

Maybe Jack feels my hesitation. He considers. He covers the trigger with his finger. There's no sympathy for the coyote. I heard the fawn's cry like Jack did. Both of us, we stepped over its still-warm body. The coyotes didn't kill Ben and Jesse. Killing the coyote won't bring them back. But the coyote—or one like him—killed the fawn, and will go on killing fawns forever. Or till there's peace in the valley, and the coyotes and fawns lie down together.

When I sense Jack stalling, I pray the coyote will move out of sight. And amazingly it does. Jack lowers the rifle. Waits. Then the coyote emerges again, something in its jaws. Rabbit? Squirrel? But no, not those. Its own pup instead.

Jack raises the rifle again.

I want to touch his sleeve, but my arms feel lifeless. Like in a dream when you want to move and can't. Want to speak and can't. But, oh, how threadbare is that jacket you wear, the one that shelters your love.

"God's place," Jack whispers. "What do you do?" He's breathing, slowly, forcing himself to breathe, the way you have to, to keep your arms and shoulders loose.

The coyote senses us because she turns to face Jack, the pup still clutched in her jaw. She's considering her options, you can tell, the way her eyes dart to and fro.

If this is to be the ram in the bushes, I pray to see it, to accept it. I throw a quick glance at Jack's face, trying to get a read on him. His eyes are wet, not even trained on the coyote, but looking inside, backwards, at how things stand. There's a lot bottled, so much bottled he don't know what to do with it.

"Let me do it," I say, reaching for his shoulder. "Or we can come back another day."

The first shot drops the coyote, maybe kills her. The second allows for no doubt. The third shot rolls the pup away from her. The shots echo through the hollow and high above us, through the trees and to the tops of the hills and beyond. The scent of gunpowder hangs in the air and sickens my heart.

"There won't be another day," Jack says, handing me the rifle. "This is it." He has his teeth clenched, his chin tight. He tucks his shaking hands in his pockets. He scrunches his eyes, nods at me, then turns away from the coyotes toward the house.

Brammer left the undertaker sitting in the hearse and climbed the hill, feeling the steepness of the incline in his legs. The men at the top were gathered around the backhoe and stood with their backs to the road. Funny how you could recognize them after so many years. There was Wetzel and Billy, Big Chew, Carl, Squirmy, Royce, Vinton. Was it that they wore the same old coats and caps? Or was it the build of their bodies, the habit of their stances that gave them away? Brammer didn't know who was on the backhoe—one of a newer generation—maybe one of Pete's sons.

Seeing Brammer, Pete waved from the top, but then turned around to supervise the digging. Most likely it was Pete who'd let news of his daddy's death slip. Pete, who'd encouraged the men to come. In small towns, people expected a funeral, a graveside service, at the least. Probably that's what he should have scheduled. But he hadn't thought he could go through with it, having to face them all and talk about his father's last months. That spiraling down until he didn't know where he was, who Brammer was, or why there wasn't an outhouse in the backyard where there needed to be one. Though he lived with Darla and Brammer his last two years, his father couldn't forget the West Virginia farm where he'd spent the rest of his life. By then, it was too late, Brammer imagined, for his father to learn about letting go. In the end, he was like a child wanting to go home. He cried for his own mother and father, wishing they would come for him, and for that perceived abandonment, so far as Brammer could tell, there was no consolation.

Still, no one could say he hadn't done right by his daddy. He had always wondered if, when the time came, he would be able to follow through. But he and Darla had cared for his daddy up to the end. Darla, really, had treated him as if he were her own father. There was nothing to feel guilty about. No regrets. He could lay his father to rest, and they could all sleep in peace this evening when the shade crawled over the Griffith family burying ground.

At the top of the hill, Brammer paused to catch his breath. There was a loud scraping in the grave, and some of the men hunched their shoulders and winced. Rock was always a problem, Brammer knew. So much so that sometimes it took dynamite to break through. But surely, they would have tried dynamite yesterday or the day before—not now with the hearse idling in the driveway.

Brammer saw Pete shaking his head and waving his arms at the backhoe driver.

"You hit rock?" Brammer yelled toward him.

"What?" Pete yelled back.

Brammer cupped his mouth and yelled louder over the machine, "I SAID DID YOU HIT ROCK?"

"WORSE," Pete yelled, then said something Brammer couldn't make out.

Pete made a short slicing motion under his throat, and the driver backed away from the grave and shut down the engine.

"It's a tractor," Pete said, a little breathless.

Brammer looked from the partially dug hole to the backhoe, trying to attach some meaning. You could call it a tractor, but technically, it was a backhoe. He felt someone's hands on his arm, turning him. It was Wetzel, shriveled up into a little old man with big ears. He nodded toward the grave, pointed to the large mound of earth still left in the wide hole.

"There's a tractor buried there," Pete said. "We been digging around it, trying to bust through the rock on the outside edges without tearing up the tractor. "But it'll take shovels to uncover it the rest of the way."

Brammer peered over the edge, straining to see into the mound of earth.

"See the top of the steering wheel?" Wetzel pointed. "And one of the fenders?"

"Whose is it?" Brammer asked.

"Whose do you think?" Big Chew asked.

Brammer glanced around at the men. He was playing catch-up—as you had to with old-timers who were always a step ahead of you. But from the tone of Big Chew's words, he knew whose tractor they thought it was.

"Dad's?"

Pete shrugged. "All my years digging graves, I never seen nothing like it."

"What makes you think it's his?"

"Don't you recognize the steering wheel?" Royce asked. Again Brammer squinted, trying to adjust his eyes to the varying degrees of earth and shadow. Had he been able to see the steering wheel, he surely would have recognized it. His father had worn the original out—worn it down to nothing—till it broke in its narrowest place, with just a hard turn one day. His father took one from an old blue Dodge they had up in the hollow, just for temporary. And then had never seen reason to replace it.

"Vinton said you reported the tractor missing a while back."

"Yeah, about a year ago," Brammer said. "I was going to have it hauled over to my place so he'd have it to tinker with." It was the truth, but Brammer said it now to win points. "Someone had already got to it," he added, then looked back down into the hole. "I don't understand why they'd bury it though."

The undertaker strode up, breathless after the climb. "What seems to be the trouble, gents?"

Pete eyed the stranger. "No trouble really. There's a tractor buried in the grave."

"Yeah, I can see it," the undertaker said.

Brammer watched him squinting his eyes, studying the earth. He wondered if he really saw it or just said he did. "They say it's my father's tractor," Brammer told him. "But I don't see how."

"Well, I'll be," the undertaker said. "That's kind of curious, ain't it? How long'll it take to dig it out?" His question fell to Wetzel, the oldest among them.

"Not long," Brammer said, cutting Wetzel off. He looked to Pete hopefully.

"There was a lot of rock around the edges," Pete said. "But we couldn't use dynamite. We had to chomp and bust it up with the backhoe. We'll have to get in there with shovels now. It's just dirt from here on."

"How'd they get the tractor down there?" Brammer asked.

"They who?" Big Chew asked.

"Whoever did it."

"Don't you know who done it?"

"How would I know?"

"You lived with him a good part of your life."

Brammer looked around at the men, their arms folded.

Brammer squinted his eyes at Pete. "Do they mean Dad?"

Pete nodded. "That's what they're claiming."

"He couldn't have done it—he wasn't able," Brammer said. "Besides, he was staying with me." By their looks, he could feel the feebleness of his protest. The jury had decided, and with them convinced against him, Brammer felt like a teenager again.

"It's been here a long time," Billy said softly. "It's all rusted out."

"So you're saying you think he buried it sometime *before* he came to live with me?" Brammer questioned. "He wasn't strong enough. It would have killed him."

"All we know, there's a tractor buried now in your daddy's plot. Been there for some time," Wetzel said. "None of us did it—or even knew about it."

"But he used that tractor for everything," Brammer said. "He didn't know he wasn't coming back—*we* didn't know. We just took him till he could get back on his feet." He felt their eyes on him. Of course, his father might have known, the way people knew things they didn't put words to. The men here might have known, too. And maybe they held it against him. In the end, when it was clear his father was going downhill, Brammer had chosen to uproot his father instead of moving himself and his wife back to the farm to care for him. He could feel the protest of the men around him. That he had a job, a life elsewhere, did not matter much. There were ways of doing things, beliefs about what things ought and ought not to be done.

Following their ears, the men turned their eyes down the drive, where the backhoe driver and another young man were already dragging shovels like sleds along the graveled ruts of the road. The shovels screeched across the quartz pebbles till the men veered off into the grass to climb the hill. When they reached the edge of the pit, they paused, looking for the best way to descend. Then they scrambled down, what seemed to Brammer, the steepest part—just what you did when you were young. They walked around the mound of dirt, studying where to start. Then one, then the other began shoveling, like they were spooning ice cream, slowly as if they meant to savor it.

Brammer tried to picture his father digging such a big hole. It would have taken him weeks—steady work at that. And how could he break through the rock? In his youth, or even in his middle years, he surely could have—he would have gotten his hands on dynamite. But at eighty-two, he wasn't able—surely he wouldn't have tried to set off an explosion—and then he would've had to do all that shoveling and lifting the rock out. When Brammer picked him up that final day, he was down to skin and bones. He trembled on the way to the car, leaning on Brammer's arm. He groaned as Brammer had never heard him groan, joints and limbs rusty in pain. At the time, Brammer wondered how his father had managed so long on his own. He regretted that he hadn't taken him sooner. And maybe he would have, if his father could have found a heart to love Darla more. But that was a sad thing that no one could do anything about.

"He couldn't have dug this hole," Brammer said. "He must have had help." He gauged the men. They met his look, then turned their gaze back to the hole.

"Brammer's probably right," Vinton said. "He must have rented a backhoe or something. A little Ditch Witch wouldn't've done it."

"Could he even operate a big backhoe?" Brammer asked.

"Clive Griffith could operate any kind of machinery," Royce said. "You oughta know that."

"One time my old man rented a bulldozer to grade around the house," Billy said. "With Daddy on it, it was hit and miss, scrape the driveway, knock down the clothesline pole, the cats flying every which way getting

out of his path. Got right up near the house—the blade stuck in midair—so that any move up or down was going to bust out the wall and
my mother standing beside the mashed clothesline pole shaking her head
and my daddy in such a sweat. Him debating over moving the dozer right
to left or left to right, and getting more and more confused about which
way the switches worked—'cause, you know, some of them work backwards—and it just got too much for him, the pressure, so he just shuts
her off, sends me out to find your daddy. I remember Clive was out cutting hay, and your mother radioed him on the walky-talky. So I come
back home, and he nearly beats me there, bouncing along on his tractor
in high gear down the road, sitting up high and pretty. Then takes the seat
in the dozer, just nudges it in reverse, pretty as you please, backs the thing
away from the house. Then after he'd fiddled with the knobs a bit, goes
ahead and grades the section up near the foundation—careful not to get
too close—he wasn't showing off none—just looked like he'd found a
new toy."

"He loved machines," Squirmy said. "He understood them."

"He liked to try out new ones," Vinton said, "but his favorite was his
tractor."

"His favorite was his tractor," Brammer repeated. "I can't see him
burying it."

Down in the hole, the shovelers had uncovered both big rear fenders—so that the tractor looked like a crouching cat, its hind legs poised,
ready to pounce.

"It was a good tractor," Squirmy said. "Wish mine was half that good."

The undertaker seemed amused. He ran his hand over the crooked
wing of his hair. "Well, now, boys, just what kind of horsepower are we
talking about?"

Brammer wished he could have warned the undertaker not to get
them started. No telling how long they'd be here if the men got started.

"It had a mighty force," Vinton said. "I can't count the times that ol'
tractor pulled my old jeep out of that creek in front of Jim McCallister's.
One time Clive give me such a jerk, the jeep went lurching forward, and I
had to mash on the brakes to keep from flying into Clive."

"Sure was a good tractor," Squirmy said again, with clear nostalgia.

"Was fast, too," Royce said. "So fast he had to rig a string around his hat to keep it from blowing off. I teased him, said why didn't he get himself a bonnet."

"Yeah, it was like he was from the Old West, that hat strapped to his chin."

"Never mind the pistols."

"Oh, I forgot about them pistols," Wetzel said. "Bet you remember them, Bram?"

Brammer smiled. They were his pistols, tucked into the handholds his father had welded on the back for him to hang onto when he was little. Eventually, he found other places to hang onto and kept his toy pistols in the handholds while they bounced along. They'd go all over the farm, from one chore to the next, or to the back door for supper. They'd ride up to his cousin Denzil's, or down to Wetzel's or over to Walton's. The men would just sit around, talking from their tractors, never get down off them. Brammer remembered going through the various yards, chasing cats and dogs with his pistols.

"Stay out of Lois's flowers," his daddy would warn him. And he'd just go on as before, maybe tiptoeing through the flowers instead of tearing through them. When he heard the tractor start, he knew it was time to go. That was the end of the visit. He'd run back and get on it.

"He sure took good care of that tractor," Billy said.

"Boy, did he."

"And that tractor took care of him," Vinton said.

It was hard to tell if the men more fondly remembered his father or the tractor.

"My old man used to say if ever there was an engine charmer, he bet Clive Griffith writ the book," Pete volunteered.

"That's saying something coming from Walton," Wetzel said. "He had his way with machinery, too. And it runs in the family—you and your boy." Wetzel nodded to the backhoe operator shoveling now in the grave.

"Don't know about that." Pete looked back at the tractor. "But my daddy was good as they come." He looked like he might say more but then simply firmed his lips.

Brammer remembered the death of Pete's father. It had been an early death, a violent death—the wind felling a dead tree, just the right place, the right angle, to kill him. The randomness of the act amazed them. It happened quickly with no warning, no time to say good-bye, and Pete's daddy was young, in his prime. Pete and Brammer were just out of high school. Brammer was home on spring break, his first year of college. He remembered the way word had come, house to house, Wetzel stopping by on his tractor, getting down off his tractor—which, in a way, maybe prepared Brammer's father. He came up the porch steps, where they were sitting. Brammer was in the rocker, his father on the swing. Brammer remembered his father's face, disbelief first, then the slow settling of restrained agony—they were good friends and wouldn't he have been out there helping Walton in the woods had he not stayed home to be with Brammer? That death had come as the Bible said, like a thief in the night, took just one, left the rest standing. But it stole their peace and security.

"They sure he's dead?" Brammer's father had asked, like it was a detail someone forgot to check.

After that, Brammer's daddy took Pete under his wing—and that made Brammer and Pete more like brothers than ever. But once Brammer started spending summers away, in between his college years, that about ended it—the camaraderie. And now that they hadn't seen each other in five years, Brammer felt shy around Pete. When you left, people assumed you thought yourself better than them. But that wasn't it at all. If anything, you felt lesser. You didn't call, you didn't visit—because you had the feeling of never making the cut, of being judged by people who didn't understand why you went off in the first place—you had property here, after all, why wouldn't you stay? At some point, it was hard to bear up under that kind of censure.

"Walt's been gone a long time," Wetzel said. "I reckon him and Clive'll have some catching up to do."

"Ain't that the truth," Squirmy said.

The men grew quiet, maybe thinking of others they knew who'd gone on. When you moved away, Brammer realized, you missed this graveside talk. But you learned to live without it, the way you learned to live without many things. And it was true, too, living away, that you began to lose touch with death. You didn't know it as intimately as you once had. It wasn't part of the weekly fabric of your life. Sure, people died all around you. But you didn't know them—or hadn't known them all your life—

and so death lost some of its sting. It was then you had to prod it periodically with your toe—the way you might check the pressure in your tires. But you went even further. You tipped it up and looked under—as if for lizards or fish worms—to keep it from mushrooming on you. In this way, it didn't swell, or envelop you in its surge.

"I can just picture Clive sitting on that tractor, out cutting hay or plowing or mowing—always mowing," Vinton said. "You'd see him from the road. Would wonder what he was going to mow next. Would mow great big patterns in his yard—checkerboards, big daisies, words even. You remember the time he mowed 'Hello' on the big hill in front of his house? Liked to never got him to mow it out."

"Not till someone come along one night, mowed out the 'o.'"

"He always thought that was the McComas boy."

"I figure it was. He never did amount to much."

"Where's he now?"

"Last I heard, camping down't McCorkle, collecting workers comp."

"Well, it wasn't for his daddy's lack of trying."

The men grew quiet, and Brammer imagined them thinking of their own sons and daughters, the best and worst of them, the ways they didn't measure up. For how could you measure up when the men carried such high standards?

"What I picture is ol' Clive pulling that old dog of his—what was his name?

"Eeensie-Weensie," Wetzel said.

"Pulling him around on that trailer. That dog went everywhere he did."

"I bet he's buried somewhere around here—I remember Clive chiseling a stone for him." Royce turned his head, searching.

"Where'd he get that name?"

"Was you, wasn't it, Brammer?" Billy asked.

Brammer nodded his head. He'd given the name when a boy. The dog had fine lines along the ridge of his back radiating out like a spider web.

Lots of the old dogs were buried here. Pets, sure, but work dogs, too, or dogs that thought they were working, always padding along behind the tractor whether it was the hoe, the rake, fence posts, or buckets of water you were hauling on the trailer. His father would be happy to see them all again—and Brammer hoped he would, hoped that Saint Francis had been right about that, and the people of other faiths and others who believed in the souls of animals. For how could you look into their eyes and *not* see a soul?

Down in the hole, the hood of the tractor was visible. Brammer could make out the steering wheel now and the shape of the round seat—like a misshapen dishpan. The tractor appeared to be emerging from an ocean, the waves dropping lower and lower around it.

"Why do we have to dig it out?" Brammer asked suddenly. "Can't we just bury Dad on the other side of Mom? And leave the tractor where it is? If he put it there, he must have done it for a reason."

"The headstone would be wrong then," Pete said. He pointed to the monument that had been dragged off to the side so the backhoe could do its work. Brammer looked at the names and dates of his parents. He forced himself to stare at the stone. It was hard to see, hard to believe. It would be up to him to have the date added to his father's side. That would be one of the final things.

"See," Pete continued. "He would be where the stone says she is, and she would be where it says he is. Unless you put it at their feet, facing the other direction. Then it would go against the direction of all the others.

Brammer couldn't see that it made much difference in the long run, but maybe it did to everyone here. He wondered what Darla would have said. She seemed distant to him now, somehow out of this orbit. He had told her it would be a short trip.

"You remember that time he was sitting on his tractor in the middle of the hay field? One of Carl Lucas's boys was coming home from Buckeye—" Vinton said.

"Was Carl's grandson, I believe," Wetzel interrupted.

"I believe you're right. Was his grandson, little bitty thing—all those boys was tiny till they got to high school and busted out. Well, Clive was sitting in the field he'd been mowing, just sitting on his tractor, engine cut off. 'What you watching?' the boy asks Clive.

"Clive puts his finger to his lips, points. He'd jumped a rabbit and her young'uns, and the rabbit and all the little ones was hopping this way and that. She was hopping ahead, trying to get them to follow, but the little

ones was just hopping ever which way. When Clive sees this ole boy of
Carl Lucas's—"

"His grandson—"

"—this grandson—Clive hops off his tractor to help the boy catch
one. They was tiny, no bigger than your fist. So the two of them was running around and around the tractor, and Carl himself comes along, says,
'Is it hide and seek, boys?' And Clive, pretty as you please, stands up with
his hat in his hand, sort of bows like, then pulls a rabbit out. Carl said in
that moment, the light came on in that ol' boy's face, said you could have
lit a baseball field by his face."

"Course you couldn't help getting them rabbits sometimes when you
was cutting hay. That was hard on old Clive then."

"Hard on any of us—especially if they had young ones. Was like
you were the grim reaper," Billy said, then turning to the undertaker, he
added, "No offense."

"None taken," the undertaker said. "I done my share of mowing. Hit
terrapins and ground-chucks and things like that. Makes you sick to your
stomach."

"I believe that ol' rabbit lived to be fifteen or sixteen, and when he died,
that ol' boy broke down and cried. You'd thought he'd lost a brother."

"Used to ride him around in a milk crate attached to the handlebars of
his bicycle, didn't he?"

Brammer remembered Russell Lucas's rabbit mainly because his father had caught one for him from the same batch. Brought it home to
him in the pocket of his jacket that afternoon. They'd put it in the empty
hamster cage—was a tiny thing. It didn't live long, though. Died the next
day. Brammer was holding it in his hand. It was squirming and struggling
so much that he thought it was getting stronger, but then it just went stiff
in his hand. He felt the life go out of it. He never forgot. The way the rabbit turned dead—the way its breath left it and didn't come back. Was no
question. And Brammer knew it. But still begged to take it to the hospital—how ridiculous it seemed now—but his father wouldn't. He blamed
his father then, and had asked didn't he love him. For years afterward, he
wished he hadn't said that. It was the kind of early heartbreak you gave
your father. And it left a sore spot in Brammer and in his father—something that got nettled—for Brammer could read it on his father's face, every time somebody mentioned Russell Lucas's rabbit.

"Well, look here," Brammer said before the men could start in on something else. "What're we going to do? Instead of digging the tractor out the rest of the way, why don't we just bury him on the other side of it. There's enough room. We wouldn't have to dig anymore."

"Then the tractor'll be laying between him and your mother," Pete said.

"They can reach across it," Brammer said. He felt himself in the undertow of their talk. "They was always reaching across it anyway—when he was working. Her offering him something for energy, a bottle of RC or a spoon of peanut butter."

"He sure liked his RC," Big Chew said.

The young men were shoveling dirt now that had been packed in tight around the tractor. There were flakes of red paint in the shovelfuls landing at Brammer's feet, and he was glad his father wasn't here to witness it.

"I just don't see the point of going to all this trouble to dig the tractor out—if he wanted it buried," Brammer said.

"I don't know. I don't know," Big Chew was shaking his head. "I suspect he don't care what we do with the tractor so long as we found it. I believe he buried it so we'd find it."

"Be kind of hard to miss, wouldn't it?" Squirmy said.

"It's like a proxy," Royce said.

"What d'you mean, a proxy?"

"You know, the person who can stand in to vote for you—something that stands in your place—in case you're not going to be there. A sub."

Brammer felt his face growing warm. There'd never been any question about where his father would be buried. It was nothing they had talked about, but was just a given. But maybe it had been something his father feared when he left the farm to come stay with him.

"It's more like a bookmark," Billy said, looking at Brammer. "Something to mark his place till he could get back."

"Well, this'll be something to tell back in Belton," the undertaker said. "It beats all I ever saw. You still hear on occasion someone taking a tractor apart, building it back in the loft or on the roof of a barn—some place unusual," the undertaker said. "But no one thinks to bury one in his grave." The undertaker seemed to be enjoying himself.

"What we could do," Pete said, "is clear out a place over on the far side of the hole like you said, Brammer, but then scoot the tractor over—all of us together—scoot it over so Clive could rest easy between your mother and the tractor."

"That all right with you, Brammer?" Wetzel asked.

"I guess," Brammer said. But he wished his father had been there to ask. What had he intended? Why hadn't he said something?

The men were down to throwing out half shovelfuls, the soil in the crevices and fine lines of the tractor. Despite the rust and so many loose paint flecks, the tractor retained some of its red color.

"That's the tractor I remember," Big Chew said. "He was always touching up the rusty spots."

"He'd sure have a job if he did it today," Wetzel said. "Would have to sand everything down to the bare metal, start from scratch."

"He didn't take much to a green tractor," Royce said.

"No, he didn't approve of John Deere. Was nothing again' the engine—but was the color that bothered him. Was like he didn't understand a green tractor."

Brammer thought of his riding lawn mower. Maybe that was his father's complaint about it. "It's not a real tractor," his father was fond of saying, in the same tone he complained that Darla's Yorkies were not real dogs. With the lawn mower, though, his father had mowed Brammer's yard every other day for nearly two years—even in the winter when snow wasn't on.

"That can't be good for the grass," Brammer had said, but his father shrugged him off. One day, Brammer found him in the neighborhood baseball field, mowing.

"How'd you get here?"

"Drove."

"On the road?" But Brammer knew the answer. That was the point when he decided to fetch his father's tractor from home. At least it would sit higher and be more visible to folks driving on the street. It had all kinds of reflective gear and flashing lights his father had rigged. But he didn't tell his father—he didn't want to get his hopes up. And it was a good thing, for when they went back to the farm and found it missing, Brammer's father had taken it hard. His father shuffled out to the barn to see for himself, then went around touching everything, putting his hands on the old logs of the barn, running his hands along the weathered planks. It was nearly more than Brammer could stand. His father stared at the rutted ground where the tractor used to sit. But he didn't say anything, just firmed his lips. Brammer thought he was blaming him, and he saw, by the light through the open door, his father's wet eyes.

But that was life, Brammer told himself at the time. You moved on—you had to. It was this ability to adapt that helped human beings survive loss—losses more awful than most of the people he knew went through. The problem with his father's generation was that they held on to everything. They couldn't let go. His mother had stored away enough leftover tin foil to cover the dome of the West Virginia capitol. And his father saved little bitty slivers of soap that were smaller than sucked candy. They had trouble throwing anything away. And it was also true, Brammer knew, with the connection they felt for each other. He understood how his father had held on and sheltered the bond with his mother for the five uneasy years after her death. Of course, that made more sense. You couldn't help but cling, the biblical word was *cleave*, to the one who shared with you your hopes and losses.

But here, in a wild—the word *ecstasy* came to Brammer—in a wild ecstasy, an uncharacteristic turn, his father had buried an old but perfectly functioning tractor. It had seen better days, sure. But what on earth would make his father do it?

"Say, what model would you say that tractor is?" the undertaker asked.

"He got it back in the sixties," Wetzel said. "How old are you, Brammer?"

"I'll be forty-eight in March."

"That's how old the tractor is," Wetzel said. "Libby was pregnant with Brammer when they bought it. Was a big deal at the time. Could they afford the payments, and the baby on the way? Was all he talked about for a while. But Clive wanted it so bad. It was Libby finally went and put a down payment on it."

"I remember him telling about that. He was scared they would lose it. Or the house one," Billy said.

"I believe it was hard for them the first years."

"Was hard for everybody."

"Always hard on anybody just getting started."

"Look," the undertaker pointed. "The big old headlights. Like frog eyes."

Even with one of the headlights broken out, the tractor had a face, and it seemed to gaze at them through its one good eye. The face was as familiar to Brammer as anyone he had ever loved.

"One time I tried to buy him a new one," Brammer said. He felt the attention of the men shift his direction. "He wouldn't hear of it. Then I was for going on and buying it behind his back. And finally Mom said, 'Even if you get him a new one, it's the old one he's going to use.' So I didn't."

"Like as not he would have warmed up to the new one," Wetzel said. "If it was from you. He'd found use for both of them. Wouldn't have wanted to hurt your feelings none. Or your mother's."

"I doubt it, boys," Big Chew said. "I give him the chance to buy my tractor at a real good price—after we quit raising a garden. He wouldn't have nothing to do with it."

"Yeah, but look at what you're talking about there," Vinton said.

Some of the men laughed. Even Brammer knew Big Chew's tractor, though bought new, was lopsided for some reason—and had a peculiar sound, when it was running, like a tea kettle. Every one of them had proposed some solution to get the whistle out—but no one, not Walt nor even Brammer's daddy could ever fix it. When Big Chew was coming to visit, everyone knew a long ways off.

"Don't much blame him myself," the undertaker said. "This is the first hearse I ever had." He pointed down the drive to where Brammer's father was lying. Brammer saw the undertaker had rolled down all the windows, and he imagined his father recognizing the breezes of home. He wondered if he minded being kept waiting. But then remembered it was by his own devising. Was that why he had done it? To keep them waiting?

"You got a son who'll take it over for you?"

"Nope. I'll be the last one. My daddy was an undertaker and his before him. But I'll be the last one. I had a boy, he got killed in a car wreck."

"That's rough," Billy said.

Brammer heard some of the men take a deep breath. He thought they were probably imagining it. For a minute, the only sounds were the slicing of the shovels, the bare metal of the shovels scraping the metal of the tractor, and the thudding of the dirt landing at their feet.

"Ain't you ever afraid of it breaking down, and you on your way to the cemetery?" Vinton asked, breaking the silence.

"Whew," Big Chew said, "and what if you were in the heat of summer? You probably ain't got no air condition."

The men recovered and laughed a little. But then, seeming to remember that one of them was lying now in the hearse, stopped short. They turned their attention to the gravediggers. The tractor had taken its old shape. The men had cleared most of the dirt away. Pete's boy brushed off a swath from the top with his forearm. It was something to see, the tractor sitting down there in the grave and, for the most part, composed. Brammer wished he had a picture of it, something to show Darla, for how could he describe to her all about it—and all that the men said, too?

"Looks like you all could use some brooms," Royce said. "Want me to get one from my truck?"

"I've got one in the back of my truck, too," Squirmy said. "Bring it, too."

With the brooms, the men made gentle sweeping motions over the tractor like they were archaeologists uncovering an ancient artifact. Brammer thought of King Tut, buried with all his treasures. So the tractor was what his father had intended to take with him? It had not been easy, he imagined, for his father to say good-bye to it. But perhaps he thought he'd be reunited with it. If his father had been on a desert island and told he could take only one thing, Brammer guessed the tractor would have been it. And why not? You used it to put out your crop and to bring in your crop. You cut your hay with it to feed your stock. On a farm, without one, you were nothing. You needed it from beginning to end.

He remembered that in the springtime, when they broke the ground, he had ridden on top of the disk behind the tractor to give it weight, so it would cut deeper. It had been, then, like a carnival ride. Around and around they'd go, the tractor pulling the disk, and Brammer laughing, his father smiling back on him, sometimes just speeding up or cutting the wheel hard, Brammer knew, to make it more fun—but not so much as to throw him off. From behind the tractor and disk would spring huge coils of earth, and out of them came fish worms hopping up, some cut in two, all of them hopping and wiggling to get back under the earth, for they were never more alive than when they'd just been uncovered. And he and his father would go along afterward, collecting them in coffee cans of dirt, saving them to go fishing.

With the tractor, his father had pulled out tree stumps, rocking back and forth, wiggling the stump, tugging it like it was a giant tooth. In the fall, they'd timbered in the woods for firewood that would serve in emergencies or on special days when you felt like having a fire. They took fallen trees mostly, ones that were seasoned—so they didn't have to cut the live ones. His father would trim off the limbs, then hook a chain around the logs and pull them down the path coming off the mountain, the logs rolling and zigzagging through the woods, ricocheting off the trunks of standing trees, jarring the leaves out of them, all the way down, and Brammer ran out in front of the tractor, in utter abandon, headlong down the hillside, heralding their coming.

On the trailer, his father had hauled buckets of water, tubs of potatoes, bales of hay. He had hauled all the dogs with all the old names—Old Skip and Rover and Billy and Tanner and Bob-Randy and Bear and Eensie-Weensie, and together with them, Brammer.

His father had taught him to drive on the tractor, then later how to plow straight rows. After he learned, his father expected it of him—even on days when Brammer wanted to be out running with Pete in the old El Camino Pete's father had fixed up. One time Brammer was supposed to plow but sneaked off with Pete. That was the time they tried smoking pot with Butch McComas under one of the big hilltop rocks up Ely, which might have made for a pleasant memory if not for what always trailed it.

When he got back to the farm, his father had lain off all the field himself, plowed it, and even sown the corn. He didn't say anything to Brammer. That was his way. He didn't say anything to him for days, just kept him locked out of his conversation. It was one of those disappointments in you your father was bound to have. And you didn't know how to make up for it. There was no way to make it up. Your father kept stubborn and locked you out. There were so many things a father would hold against you when you were just making your way in the world, when you were just seeking joy and then later, too, when you had found your own steadfast sustenance.

"Say, guess what?" one of the young men yelled from the grave of the tractor. "He left the key in it."

"Give it a try," Vinton said.

"Nah." The man frowned. "There's probably not even gas in the tank."

"Like that'd be the main concern," Squirmy said.

"Let Brammer try it."

"Yeah, Brammer. You go try it."

Brammer shook his head. "It won't start," he said. "After all this time—and out in the weather, rain seeping down, rusting away." He glanced at the men to make sure they were joking, but they looked serious. That was just how they would look, leading you along. He had never really acquired the ability to read them, and he wondered if Pete had. He looked at Pete now for some sign.

"Go on," Pete said. "You may's well try before we cover her back up next to your daddy."

So Pete was one of them now. Brammer didn't like being put on the spot, but he wanted to do right by his father. He looked at the men again. Wetzel nodded toward the grave. "Go on down there," he said.

Brammer swallowed. His heart was beating hard, and he felt himself breaking into a sweat.

"It's all right," Billy encouraged him. "For old time's sake."

Sometimes the right thing was going along with them even when you knew what they were up to. Brammer started down the side of the hole and felt the loose earth slipping into the tops of his shoes. He knew very well that the tractor wouldn't start. Maybe they would laugh at his gullibility. Maybe that's what they would tell stories about at the next funeral, how he got down in the pit to start his father's tractor that had been seizing up and rusting more than two years in the grave. He knew it wouldn't start, but he didn't mind getting a closer look anyway.

He approached the tractor as if it were a strange horse, slowly, holding his hand out to it, in friendship. He could see the rusty brake pedals—pads long worn off, the clutch pedal—what was nothing but a rod, the paint worn off decades ago. All the pedals were rusty now—no boot soles to keep the rust at bay. And here was the big dent, the bent fender where Brammer had one time backed his father's truck into it because he had backed without looking in the rearview mirror. His father had been disappointed that day, too. And Brammer had cried—even though he was too old to cry—but he had felt the too-great weight of the violation.

On the tractor he saw the handholds his father had welded for him, and just barely he could make out the rust-swollen pistols—welded now, whether by his father or by time, as permanent fixtures. Brammer switched his gaze to the steering wheel, for it was too much to look at the pistols. But he would remember them and tell Darla.

When he touched the blue-vinyl steering wheel, he felt the first wave topple the flood wall. He sensed what was coming and knew there was nothing now left to stop it—it had been set in motion by the pistols and by the tractor and by the memories of the men, and now it spun closer. Most likely, the men had set him up. They had herded him into a chute where there was no place to go but straight through. He reached for the key with his right hand. The key ring was corroded and snapped in two at the touch of his fingers. But the brass key itself was firm between his forefinger and thumb. Leaning his wrist clockwise, he turned the key in the ignition and was surprised at its turning at all.

There was a click and then nothing. Nothing took hold. Nothing registered. There was no spark. No turn over. No intake. No anything. But in the silence, Brammer heard the familiar chug-chug-chug and chortle of the tractor starting. It turned over in his heart, and he felt it saturate him, the sound of the day starting, the goats waiting to be let out of the barn, the tractor puttering forward, the dogs all bounding toward it determined to go wherever it was going, the throttle increasing, and you were late to it and had to get running—ground to break, rows to plow, corn to sow, all of it starting without you, but starting, and you could run to catch it if you were fast enough.

It started in his abdomen and worked its way upward—not nausea nor faintness but heat, rushing heat, and he felt it rushing and overtaking him. He swallowed and clutched the steering wheel and blinked, trying to push it back but felt a hard sob escape, and others, lined up behind like waves on a shoreline. He knew the men were watching him, but he couldn't stop. He gripped the steering wheel tighter and leaned his head down on his arm. He longed for the comfort of Darla, the way she cradled his head, the consolation of her hand on his neck, her silent but strong presence when silence and strength was what he needed. What had they been thinking, when they decided she wouldn't come?

He heard the men mumbling and moving about. Would they leave him in the grave alone with his grief? When he looked up, he saw them climbing down, some sliding, one or two jumping into the pit. The undertaker was helping Wetzel. For just a second, Brammer thought it was the tractor they were coming for, but then he felt the solid grasps and pats of their hands on his shoulders and the circle of their arms around him.

CROSSING WITH SASSAFRAS

A goat that a fellow can see through is better than no goat at all. That's how I've come to think of it. With Emma and the children gone, Sassafras will be good company—even though her flying unnerves me. She jigs through the autumn air this morning, lighter than a cloud, her pink udder swaying side to side, flapping against her spindly legs, which jerk and propel her past me, sometimes within a hair's breadth. Her hot, grassy breath comes quickly, like she's anxious even, making me believe that if I leaned in close, didn't try to dodge her, she'd tell me a secret, something I want to know. But I haven't found the courage to stand my ground as a man ought, to not flinch when she gallops by so near. The times when I've gathered up my strength, tried to coax her to me, she keeps her distance.

Ever since she showed up, I've been mending her fence, and today, I'm at it again. It's not that I think she'll stay put. I mean, if the fence didn't hold her while she was alive, I can't expect it to keep her ghost. Then why get out and labor and sweat for a lost cause? you will ask. The answer is simple: I want her to know that a goat's ghost is welcome here, can stay as long as there's weeds to trim, bark to gnaw on, tender redbud leaves to chew and swallow and belch up later.

But putting a fence back together is a job for a young man. I'm not as stout as in the days when I chased her and the others back to the fence every time Emma found them in the garden. With my fingers, I trace the braided, rusty wire between barbs and remember the coarse white hair

I used to find snagged here—evidence of Sassafras passing through. I reach for my handkerchief to soak up the sweat on my head, a trickle under my nose. My fingers streak the handkerchief with gritty rust. I wave this, an orange-and-white truce flag, at the nanny goat ghost, and for a minute she makes like she will bolt but stays put over by the water well, wagging her head.

From my shirt pocket, I pull out a long peppermint piece, peel off the sticky wrapper, and try to draw her to me. Sassafras doesn't budge. But at least she's got her hooves on the ground for now. She stares at me like the pasture isn't green enough for her, and it puts me in the notion to just walk away and be done with all her blurry whiteness. But it's that habit she has of looking back over her shoulder, to some distant point in the field, that grips. It's not the first time she has held me so, spellbound.

"Stop her! Obert—Obert," Emma yells for me. "Stop her. Obert! Where are you?" I've been two hours in the sun-striped stall of the barn, dung to my knees, shoveling flaky manure onto the trailer of my tractor, hearing clump after clump thud in the trailer bed. Despite the handkerchief Emma makes me wear over my face, dust still clots in my nostrils. But even so, I'm happy to take manure dust any day over the soot I breathed in the Buckeye Hollow Mine that one summer working for Emma's father. I choked down that fine coal powder only a month, but I never forgot the gritty dust that laid cover to everything, that burrowed its way under the elastic of your clothes like chiggers and rubbed you raw, that burned in your throat, grated in your teeth, hours after you'd left the hole in the earth.

"Stop her! Stop her, Obert!"

I step around the heaped trailer, and the warm, moist March air soothes my throat. The fullness of the sun takes away my vision a moment before I catch sight of Sassafras coming toward me, her mouth full of dishrag. Her neck cranes far around, looking back at Emma. All the while the goat walks stiff-legged, defiantly, jerking her legs like she's marching. Coming straight for me.

"Obert," Emma says and stops and stamps her feet. Emma. Catch your breath, this, seeing her again. Catch your breath. "Obert! You take this goat on over to Delano Burton's. I don't ever want to see her again. Do you hear me? Do you understand? It's not enough she eats my garden all summer long, but now she's made a meal of my clean wash, too. It's more than a body can stand."

Sassafras hides behind me. I feel her there, warm flank against the back of my legs. Hear her loud breathing too. Emma drops her hands. "I'm too old to have to be chasing a goat all over creation," she says. "It was different when we were young. Can't you keep her penned in that fence you're always working on?"

Emma swings a poplar switch at her side, and I guess this proves too much for the white nanny. I hear her gagging, feel the ground jar behind me, feel scraping against the back of my boots. I turn to find her lying in the grass, spinning, her head rocking to and fro, eyes large, bright, a choking deep in her throat. The dishrag has vanished. Forcing her jaws, I reach for it, but it's too far gone for me to get a good hold.

"Get my pliers from the garage, from the bucket on the bench, blue-handled ones, long-snouted ones," I yell to Emma. I hold the quivering goat head in my lap, watch her glassy eyes roving to sky to grass to me and around again. How I have hated witnessing it, impending panic, each and every time. Her milky body stirs, then does not stir, life, still, but escaping out her fragile edges. "It's okay, girl," I tell Sassafras. "It's okay. Don't worry."

"Emma, hurry with the pliers," I whisper under my breath. "I'm losing her. Emma, hurry, hurry, hurry, hurry. Emma, here to me. Here to me, hurry. As fast as you can. Hurry now."

"Don't worry about supper," I tell Emma. "Just turn off the fire under the beans. The curtains are fine. It's almost dark. Hurry. I *did* lock the doors."

Emma. That month gone from you was a long time, not knowing when I would be back, if ever I would be. On Buckeye, they told me those deep, black tunnels have a way of burying a man's own deep things, of making him forget, deny what's most important to him. You give it all up every time you go down. But I remembered you. I never forgot. Hurry. Your neck, sweet, sweet neck, the delicate nape. Let me touch your neck there, where your hair trails off, swirls, barely wisps. Let me hold my face flush against your face. Do you hear me not breathing? Did you hear the air leave? I'm nearly afraid to touch you. But I do touch you. And cradle your neck in my hand. My face here, Emma, and the soft scent of your skin. I dreamed of your neck in the camps at night. And remembered it and remembered it, remembering it against my face and under my lips, crawling in the tunnels every morning where I could not breathe for the dust. This, all of you. And don't hurry now. Home, to this length of you, against me. Fabric going away, your bare skin. I'm not breathing. Stifled beside you. My face hard pressed against your warm shoulder, I cannot even form my lips to kiss, my mouth, limp, open, against the flesh of your neck. Do you groan? Emma. Emma. I have known you forever. I have never not known you. Emma.

I narrow my eyes to the misty image before me, the nanny goat ghost in the tall, crisp horse weeds that've grown all around and up through the old wooden trailer of my tractor. She sighs, a delicate "mmeheh," and continues chewing her cud. She scrapes her hoof on the lowered end of the trailer like she's trying to get my attention, like she wants maybe to go for a ride—or like maybe she wishes the children were here, wants to pull them in the trailer the way the other goats did when the children were little. She's about ten feet away, keeping herself out of range of the short-handled hatchet I've been hammering and prying on the fence with. I see the brisk swats of her short tail, batting flies, and hear her steady, slow munching in the quiet of this place. I look around, take a slow sweep of the land, see the horizon wobble a little, move away and come back to me. I wipe my eyes and put the handkerchief back in my pocket.

The earth wobbles again and my head swims. I flip over the tin bucket that hauls my mending tools and sit down. In my deep pockets, the steeple nails scratch my thighs, and I shift my britches so they won't hurt. There's crimson crust on my arm where barbs have caught my skin.

I feel my heart beating fast and hard and close to my throat and wonder if I've overdone it. It's those pills that make me dizzy, the ones the doctor prescribes, pills the children make me promise to take, day in, day out, week after week after week. Before them, I was strong, but now I'm not. They're the same heart pills that took Emma. She told me they made her heart jitter and quake. But I said, "It's something you've been eating, Emma." She said they made her forget things and imagine things that never happened. I said, "Take them. They're for your own good. Take them if they keep you here with me longer." She wanted that, I know as sure as I'm sitting here. But it's been ten years since the pills ate up her heart. Had I been in my right mind, had it not been such a jolt then, maybe I would have started taking them the day she died, the day she stumbled in the garden, panting for air, after we'd picked bushel baskets and buckets of beans and scooted them onto the plywood trailer, its onion-smooth tires sinking deeper in the dirt with each full basket. I remember how she wanted me to take the beans to the house and come back for her with the trailer. She didn't think she could walk. But I knew not to wait and made room for her between the baskets. She wouldn't let me leave any of the beans behind for fear Sassafras would gobble them down. And maybe she would have.

I pull out the handkerchief again and wipe my eyes. Why is Sassafras here—back from the grave? I treated her right. All of us did, even Emma. Did she just get lonesome? Fixing her fence, I haven't made it fifty feet from the barn, and from my bucket seat I survey the line ahead of me, the wire that's been wrenched from termite-whittled posts, some strands now burdened under the weight of a twisted, uprooted willow. It seems an impossible task.

Suddenly Sassafras lifts herself off the ground—like she's a giant bird, yet without wings. She sighs her familiar "mmeheh" and goes back to chewing, suspended there between earth and sky. The grass squeaks in her mouth, and periodically, she stops chewing and looks behind her, away over the eerie field like she's expecting someone. I look behind her, too.

Emma rushes, the blue-handled pliers in one hand, the other clutching her blouse at the top to keep it from flying open while she runs. "Here, hurry," she says, crouching beside me.

"You pull the dishrag out," I say. "I'll hold her jaws apart. You pull it out."

"I'm afraid," Emma says. "Maybe I should call Michael. It wouldn't take him long to get here."

"Don't be afraid. Just grab a hold when I open her jaws. Pull gently, not fast."

Sassafras is motionless now, without struggle. The goat's eyes are wide and rolling. I pry, careful not to disjoint her jaws, saliva on my hands, opening, holding open with all my strength. I am shaking. Emma moves her hand, pliers clasped, into the sticky muzzle, further now, and with a good hold, she pulls gently. She pulls slowly, more and more red and white checkers appearing, wet, grassy even. We smell the inside of the goat, a bitter, rotting scent from one of her cavernous stomachs. She gags deep in her throat. They gag, both of them now gagging, and Sassafras coughs, kicks, with the dishrag out, kicks around and whirls herself up, no prisoner, stands coughing, her head down very low and each long, deep cough lifting her off the ground.

"I was afraid we lost her," Emma says and leans against me, and my nose brushes hers, hot tears on her face. Emma. I couldn't have risked missing this, not being here. I couldn't have gone back to the mine. It was harder on us this way, with your father's disappointment, and not the money we could have had, the nice cars other men had, the machines that would have made things easier for you in the beginning. I couldn't risk not seeing you again, my eyes filling with the night, the earth swallowing me. I never regretted buying my ticket home, even when I couldn't meet the eyes—eyes so white—of the other miners.

I look at the goat ghost, floating now, about two feet above the ground, above the upended trailer, staring past me to the house. I wonder if she's going to fly at me again.

When I hear Emma call that lunch is ready, I swivel on my bucket, my legs stiffening as I try to straighten up. Standing makes my heart beat faster again. She'll probably worry that I'm getting another goat since I've been working on the fence. Will I tell her Sassafras has come back? I picture her watching from the kitchen, scouring dried egg from dishes, muttering to herself, muttering about me out here pouring honey in the pasture. Of course, Sassafras would have nothing to do with the golden, oozing stream—though it used to be a treat for her. When I saw it was so, I wiped the rim of the jar with my forefinger and licked it, screwing on the cap. It takes patience to win a goat. I've always known that.

Inside the house I wash up. The kitchen is empty, and I remember Emma is not here, hasn't been here in a long time. I open a couple of cabinets stocked with the corn, tomatoes, pickles, and peach preserves that Katie's been canning. On the counter she's left a jar of green beans, though she knows I don't eat them now. Emma could grow them any-where. Here on the kitchen floor if she wanted. She had a way with them. Slaved to save as many as she could, weeding, and picking, stringing and snapping, washing, her hands in the cool water, fingers sifting, straining them, packing them in quart jars. Thump, thump, thump, the jar on a towel-softened counter, she made them settle tight.

Straight from Buckeye, off the train, with my bag of sooty clothes slung over my shoulder, I've scrubbed myself as much as I could. From outside the screen door on the porch, I watch her. Her elbows bend at right angles over the counter. There's deliberation in all her movements, all of it from memory, having done it so many times before, and the back of her neck, arched now, catches light as she reaches for another jar. The light stays there, a sign. I wasn't made for the dark as some men. I couldn't risk losing this, leaving her, not for any amount of money or her father's good opinion. I wanted every night of my life to be beside her. There wasn't time to waste, not even in the beginning.

How long I watch I don't know. I knock. I'm weak in the knees, all my joints watery. She dries her hands, throwing the dish towel over her shoulder. Backing from the kitchen counter, reluctant to leave, she turns to the door like she doesn't want to be disturbed. But then she says, "You, Obert!" The door swings out far, she fills my arms, just fits there, bouncing up and down, rocking me. Emma, you are lovely. I am not breathing, you are tight around me, tight inside my arms, every muscle straining to be closer, my face brushing your neck. I am not breathing. I am holding you inside my lungs and not breathing. Smile at me. Emma. What? You say, "We have so many green beans this year."

I warm some leftover potatoes and cream corn from the refrigerator and scoop them onto a plate. The jar of green beans I put on the table too. While I eat, I run a finger along the cold glass of the jar, the "Ball" lettering. I pick it up to feel the weight. I haven't eaten green beans in ten years. She could make them grow anywhere. But when she died, I tried growing a patch in the garden, just a small one, because I loved them so. Not a single split-seeded vine broke through the earth, and I knew I would never eat them again.

"Obert, will you be having any green beans this evening? There are so many," Emma says. "Did anyone have green beans, where you were, at the camp? When you came out of the mine in the evenings? I put lots of bacon in them, just the way you like them." Her hair is up because I keep going on about how happy I am to look at her lovely neck, to bury my face against her neck. I've been asleep, and my clothes are scattered on the floor. The sheets are full of her scents, and above that, on another level, I smell the green beans cooking in the kitchen. My stomach growls. I watch her move around the room in her slip, unpacking my bag, holding my gritty shirt close to her face where the black mixes with her tears.

"Will you go back?" she asks.

"They can't pay me enough, Emma," I say. "I know they're others who like the money, especially when there's none to go around. But I'll see that we get by, I promise. Tell your daddy thanks and all, and not to worry. We'll get by."

I wait for her to say something, but she only smiles, looks at me.

"I've thought about it a lot," I say. "Do you think we could raise goats, Emma?" She squints her eyes like she's trying to better understand me.

"We could sell the milk, butter, cheese," I say. "Probably not much in it but a little something." I prop myself up on my elbows. "Emma, when I was down there, eating lunch on my back, no such thing as light, I could see them, all white goats, on our hillside, against the green of our hillside. We had them when I was a boy, Emma. Would you like that?" She comes to me across the bed, nestles in my arms, lowering her head on my chest so I can nestle my face against her shoulder. I think of her, my princess in the pasture, with white goats all around her flowery skirt.

I've eaten without savoring, have lifted my fork twenty, maybe thirty times without realizing or remembering. The pills make me forget so easily. When I stand, I take the head-swim again, blood gushing up there around my brain to the front of my eyes. Suddenly I feel overcome, having the goat ghost on my hands, zinging by my head occasionally, in and out of the house, Emma not around to help me chase her back to the pasture. I move to the bedroom, crumple on my bed, atop the covers. My body unfolds easily, smooths itself out.

I dream but find I am awake with Sassafras sailing about in the room, legs kicking this way and that, her pink udder swinging. Slowly I rise so as not to spook her. She moves like she's not flying but rather running in the air, leaning in as she cuts corners in the room. Come here, girl. Come down from there. We've got to go outside. I reach for her, thinking my hand will go through her, but I catch hold of her slim hind leg, the crook where her skin is thin. She yanks, but I don't let go and sense that she is lifting me from the floor, and I am flying too. She pulls me higher, and when it looks like she will go through the ceiling, I turn loose and fall flat on the bed, almost in a daze.

"Mmeheh," she says, and goes dashing through the wall. I see her then out under the sugar maple, on the ground, looking behind her. Maybe I could call Michael to help me lock her in the barn tonight. But what will he say?

When I finally go back out to catch her again, the evening air is chilly, and the shadows of the hills are long. I pick my way out to the pasture, the goat a few steps ahead of me. I have a cinnamon roll and peppermint pieces for her, and at the pasture I offer them, but she won't come close to me now.

Emma's chased her from the bean vines, where she feasted all morning and now she won't forgive me. Neither of them will forgive me.

"She probably consumed fourteen quarts," Emma tells me. "That's fourteen meals when we could have eaten beans this winter, but your goat got them," she says. My eyes follow the direction of her finger, upper end of the garden, the white goat peering through the cornstalks.

"What will you do?" Emma asks. She picks up dirt clods and runs at Sassafras. Yelling, she throws them, and clouds of dust burst all around the goat. Sassafras waits until the very last minute, getting every bite she can, then turns on her heels and runs, cutting in and out of the rows of the garden so tenderly cared for, heading away and then back until she tricks Emma off balance, gets past her and runs to me, like I will save her. But she sees I'm braced to catch her, and when I dive, finding the hard, dry earth smoking in my teeth, she slips through my arms. Emma is over me.

"Get up, get her, Obert. Get that goat."

"Don't run, Emma, you'll scare her, walk slowly." I stalk the goat then, matter-of-factly, with her doing that stiff-legged trot she does, the pink of her behind shining under her raised tail, her looking over her shoulder, back at Emma. "Here, Sassafras, come here, girl. I won't hurt you," I say. "Come here, girl."

Sassafras leads me up the overgrown path. The horseweeds slap my face, and I feel their coarse edges, brown from frost. The air is cool. She stays only a few feet ahead, like she knows I move slower these days. Soon enough, the going gets easier. Through the pine forest where the needles are orange, fiery orange this evening with the sun so low, we go. Around us are the twisted, crackling bushes, twined with dying catbriers. She mounts the hill, a youthful goat. I see her legs pushing off the ground, each strong step to take her higher. And now she leaps over the pushed-down fence, with the same ease she had when it was a good fence. She leads me over the crest to the family cemetery.

"You can't bury her there, Dad," Katie says to me. "What will people say?"

"But she's part of the family," I say. "She's been a friend to me."

"Bury her somewhere else—behind the barn maybe," Michael says.

"It's a private cemetery," I say. "No one comes here, no one will ever know there's a goat buried here. It's not like I'm going to buy a monument for her or anything. I'll just carve her name on a rock. She's been with me so long and given me reason to get up in the mornings after your mother died, after I got her home in the trailer that day and before I could even lift her from it, when she could not catch her breath."

"Breathe slowly," I said, "please, hold on, breathe slowly now." Her eyes were wide. "I don't want to leave you, I don't want you to leave, please, breathe slowly, in and out, in and out." My hand is under her head, cradling her neck, wet and hot. "Hold on, I'll call the children, hold on, they'll hurry, they will be here, we'll get you to the hospital, hold on, Emma, breathe, I am with you, don't be afraid, please, breathe, breathe, please, please, please."

Her eyes are far brighter than in life, wide open, taking in everything, or maybe nothing. "Emma, please, you're not breathing. You're not trying. Please breathe."

"Let me stay with her," I tell the ambulance driver. "She's scared, please save her, give her back to me, please. Emma. Let me hold her hand."

"Take my hand, Dad, while we walk there," Katie says. "Mom will rest there. She'll be okay, happy on this hill, near the pasture, not too far from the garden she loved."

"It's not an easy walk," I say. I've walked it hundreds of times, checking the fence, mending the gaps, but it seems like today I can't bring myself to walk it. They carry her slowly, steadily. Sometimes they slide in the red mud. Their arms are tense. They don't want to drop her. Seems like my feet are going without my moving them. At the graveside, they would leave the coffin on top like that, wait for me to leave, to turn my head. It doesn't make sense to me. Seeing a thing done means seeing it done.

"I'm not leaving," I tell them. "Be done with it, boys."

"Dad, walk back with me."

"You don't understand," I say. "Let me be." It doesn't take long, not long at all, once they've lowered her into the earth. Their shoulders and elbows bending, they send the red dirt through the air. It thuds below at first but then just falls softly and silently, and finally they're ready to leave. They think I'm going to be a hard case. But I'm not. I just want to be left alone with her. "Go on home," I say. "I want to be alone. Come back for me if it makes you feel better, just leave me here a while. I'll be ready when you come back."

I don't want to be alone, please, Emma. After that first month away, I never left again. I could not. You know that. We were never apart again.

"I will not leave you," I tell her, the bean juice sticky on my chin. "You never leave me either, you hear, Emma."

"Why would I?" she says, snuggling close. "You're my world."

The shoveling done, men gone, I can't wait for anyone to come back and I leave the mound, the place they've put Emma. At the fence, on her side for once, Sassafras—she knows. Through the fence I touch her pink nose.

"Mmeheh," she says.

"Mmeheh," I repeat. I walk up a ways to the gate and enter the pasture to be with her. We walk back together. Not wanting to go home but not wanting to go anywhere else either. She picks at a leaf here and there, but that's all. Like me, she's not hungry.

She leads me past the cemetery, high up on Mark's Knob, to that steep place. I know she's going to fly. I know it. I want to catch her at that moment, to stop her before she leaps up. I want to bring her home with me, tie her to the poplar in the yard till I get the fence fixed, keep her from going away from me again. I crawl on my hands and knees now and feel the earth under my palms. I scoot toward the edge where she pauses to look back over her shoulder—but not at me, past me.

"Mmeheh," she says. Her cry is urgent. She stares past me but I see nothing unusual. I reach for her as far as—reach—all of me stretching—another inch or—all my—this—is all—to grab hold of her, to clutch her to myself. My fingers find her coarse hair, joint of her hind leg, almost within my grip. All the way. Emma, I have her. She's lifting off the ground. I have her, I will, I have her this time. But my hand is slipping, I can't hold on much longer, she is, I am, slipping, and I lose hold, fall, am rolling, down the hill. I go down, sliding and rolling, with the earth and leaves blurry fast in front of my face. Until it all stops, and my body curls inward to the burning pain.

I look up at the sky, see the ghost goat hovering above the persimmon trees. Can't she see I want her to stay, that there's room here for her? I stand up, my head reeling. Sassafras floats out of sight, leaving me behind. I brush off my clothes and head toward home. Emma will be worried, will have supper on the table waiting for me, maybe even her green beans this evening.

"Emma," I say, entering. "I'm home." But there's no answer and I guess she's running late. I don't know when she'll be home, and I figure I'll have to cook the beans for us. I wash my hands and pop open the lid of the jar with a can opener. Dump them into a pot on the stove and turn the fire on. I wash the day's dirty dishes while they heat up. I'm tired and I wish Emma would get home soon to eat supper. It's not like her to be gone anywhere this late.

Through the window I see Sassafras perched in the sugar maple—aglow. I can't tell if she's standing on a branch or just floating at the moment. It's too much for an old man like me, having a crazy goat who doesn't know whether she's beast or bird. I keep my eye on her, and when the beans are ready, I lift about five tablespoons into a dish for me and three into a dish for Sassafras. I set hers on the floor, trying to lure her into the house while Emma isn't here. I put the lid on the pot so the beans will stay warm till Emma gets back.

Back through the dark house I go with my beans. In the bedroom, Sassafras surprises me, having come through the wall. Her glow lights the room. Emma will not be happy about having a goat in the house, but Sassafras needs a place to stay until I finish the fence. I'll just have to explain it. On the bed, I pull the blankets over me and lie back. With my fingers, I eat the beans. They're fine in the way they're always fine, and I keep nibbling at them, trying to savor each one, figuring they'll tide me over till Emma's home for supper.

The dish is warm, is heaped high, green beans and a strand or two of bacon threading through, on my bare chest, warm, the dish, when you feed them to me, one at a time, with your fingers, picking one and putting it in my mouth, watching my face, waiting till I swallow before reaching for another, every green bean on the plate this way, and occasionally, one wrapped with a shred of limp bacon, until the dish is empty and there's just the juice then, which you drain into my mouth, down my chin, across my chest, that you kiss clean.

Sassafras never eats them hot because they burn her mouth. But she likes them cold, cooked or raw. When she takes sick, I bring some candy to the stall where she lies, thinking it might help her. She eats it all from my hand, careful, as she always has been, not to bite my fingers. She eats everything I bring today but tomorrow she won't. She doesn't stand now. There are no more bowel movements. She coughs. When she begins the loud, gut-wrenching bellows, I know what will have to happen.

"Maybe we can call a doctor," Katie says. "Or Delano Burton. He'll know what to do."

"She's very old," I say. "She's suffering. I'll hitch up the trailer, carry her back on the hill, and we'll put an end to it." Emma's been gone four years, so it's the children, Michael and Katie, who help me lift her, mmehehing, mmehehing, to the trailer.

"You ride back here with her," I tell them. But they don't want to. They are grown now.

"I can't do it, Dad," Katie says. "I can't."

"I can't either," Michael says. "Shouldn't we call the vet? Get him to give her a shot?"

"One of you will have to drive the tractor then," I say, "and I'll ride with her. You can leave before I do it." Emma would have stayed with me, would have known what it required—and would have been my help.

Beside the grave, just at the boundary of the cemetery, a place where no one else would want to be buried, I give her peppermint. The children leave, don't even look back over their shoulders. I watch them as long as I can and turn back to Sassafras, who drops the peppermint from her mouth. My jaws are so tight they hurt, my throat knotted like I might vomit. I pet her head, run my hand gently on her floppy ears. "Mmeheh." She is swollen and cannot stand. She cries out at all hours. She is fourteen, a ripe age for a goat, one we thought would die a day old. When the mother died, Emma fed her formula with a nippled RC bottle, named her Sassafras, and the tiny kid ate, punching her nose at the nipple, milk bubbles foaming at the sides of her mouth, her tail spinning, spinning. You cradle her as one of your own, Emma, as me even, soothing her head, your fingers soft and strong, scent of green beans on them, taste of them, passing over my lips, the edges of my teeth.

The gun is nothing but weight and cold. It has always seemed so to me. You never asked me to do it, would never have, no matter how many beans Sassafras ate. But there isn't a choice now. She won't get up again. I've seen it too many times with all the other goats. You have been gone from me four long years. You were my strength. Just to have you again, Emma. That last day, losing you.

I aim, but not I, someone else, at her head, not her head, there, just a target, I pretend, and squeeze. One shot. Then a second. They shouldn't let me do it. I'm no good with a gun, have never been, have made a mess of it. And am too old. I don't have the stomach. Didn't even as a young man. They haul that miner up, pulling him out on a rail cart, mangled. He's one of the lucky ones, someone says. At least they got his body. I don't know him, so it isn't that. You just never know when you go under if you'll see daylight again, or the other things that light your life. His wife is soaked in the rain, a scarf pasted to her head. When she sees his body, so pale and broken, she reaches, knees going, her head bowed, her neck, a flash of your head bent, the back of your neck catching light, while you string beans. I couldn't go down there again. I walked away the same hour and bought my ticket home. Some men get over it or get used to it, your daddy told me. But I thought my train to you would never come.

My skin is cool, damp from sweat tonight. The cold dish lies empty on my chest. It's dark all around. Momentarily, I close my eyes, stilling myself, quieting my heart, while I wait. When I open my eyes, Sassafras is on her way down again, bright as day, pulling a trailer out of the sky. She looks behind her, away off in the distance toward the bean patch where Emma stands, waving, yelling that it's supper time. Sassafras comes closer and closer, trotting her stiff-legged gait, finally swinging the trailer down within reach. When she halts in front of me, I hoist myself up and climb on board to go.

CPSIA information can be obtained
at www.ICGtesting.com
Printed in the USA
BVHW07s0916250918
528439BV00002B/566/P

9 780820 354729